JACK

TUCKER'S PRIDE BOOK 4

KATHI S. BARTON

This is a work of fiction. Names, characters, places, and incidents are products of the author's imagination or are used fictitiously and are not to be construed as real. Any resemblance to actual events, locations, organizations, or persons, living or dead, is entirely coincidental.

World Castle Publishing, LLC
Pensacola, Florida

Copyright © 2025 Kathi S. Barton
Hardback ISBN: 9798311278522
Paperback ISBN: 9798891263529
eBook ISBN: 9798891263536
First Edition World Castle Publishing, LLC, February 18, 2025
http://www.worldcastlepublishing.com

Licensing Notes

Cover: Cover Designs by Karen
Editor: Karen Fuller

Prologue

Taylor watched as two men struggled with a walker across the lawn from them. She didn't know if it belonged to either man as the thing had balloons and a very festive bag on the front to carry things in. Wondering aloud if they'd stolen it — or had borrowed it from someone at the retirement center.

"Those old fools. Look at them out there acting like bullies. Mr. Reglan will fight someone over the last pea on his plate and then say you stole it from him. Mr. Martin isn't all that much better. They squabble like small children when I know for a fact that both of them are in their late seventies." Turning to look at her grandmother, really her great-grandmother, she smiled. "They should have been beaten more as children and — yes, I said it. Had their bottoms beaten more as children, and then they'd know how to properly act around their elders."

"Mom beat my bottom a great deal. I still

have no manners around my elders." Grandma huffed at her. "I was just thinking about breaking you out of here so we can have some fun. You remember fun, don't you? Or is watching rude old men without underwear on more your cup of tea."

"Oh, dear lord. They neither one have underwear on." Grandma turned away just as one of the people who worked there rescued not just the walker but the men as well before they exposed themselves too much more. "What would possess a person to walk around in that kind of gown. We all have clothing that we brought with us—is that your mother coming up the walkway? Taylor, I have no patience for her today. If she asks me more than one time if I'm all right, I'm going to brain her with my cane. I think I will anyway." Laughing, Taylor greeted her mom and her new fling.

Her mom told her that she was experiencing life again. That meant that she was dating everyone that she came in contact with who wasn't married. Divorced was all right, but she'd not be responsible for breaking up a marriage she'd told her when she was old enough to understand that her mom was lonely.

Taylor supposed that her mom's lesbian

phase was going on right now. Not that it bothered her; her mother was a grown woman, and she loved her to pieces. Taylor just wished her mom would settle down and not be so odd all the time.

"Hello, Mom. Jeri. How are you guys feeling?" Grandma tsked at her while her mom went on and on about what the two of them had been up to today. "I didn't realize that the winery was open this time of year? Or did they just open? It's hard to keep up sometimes."

Her mom, Gilda Jane, had been widowed at a very young age. Her dad, Henry Paul Murphy, had had a massive heart attack at the age of forty-three. Leaving mom and her, at only six weeks old, to fend for themselves.

It really wasn't all that bad. They didn't ever have to beat down the debt collectors or anything like that. It was just that. They were alone in a hostile world that her mom had never understood. No, she told herself, her mom had never wanted to understand. If her grandma hadn't taken them in when she did, Taylor didn't know what would have happened to them. Her mom was as flighty as she'd ever met.

"How are you feeling, Harriette? Are they feeding you well?" Grandma, not hard of hearing, winched with each word that mom would shout at her. "I hope you're getting enough rest."

"Mom. You do this every time. She can hear you just fine. More than likely better than you hear. Sit down and tell us what you're doing here. This isn't your usual visit day." Mom settled in next to her, leaving her friend and companion sitting on the ground. Mom asked her how long she'd been here. "Since ten. Grandma and I are going to break out today and go get some supper."

"Aren't you afraid she'll get away?" She told her mom to behave herself. "I am. I don't know what she's like when we're not here. They probably keep her drugged up or something to keep her this calm."

"I'm right here, so stop talking about me as if I'm not. And I can hear you just fine, Gilda Jane." Grandma rolled her eyes before speaking again. "Didn't you know that they hook us up to all kinds of tubes when no one is around? Yes, sir. And they have probes everywhere on us. Every orifice has one, too. And we're not to complain or they take one of our toes off. See that man over there with his foot all wrapped up. It's because he questioned them one night. Messy thing—"

"Now, who should be behaving. Grandma,

you can't tell Mom that. She believes you." And it looked as if she had, too. "They don't put tubes in your orifices either. Behave, or I'll make you have liver and onions for dinner."

"It just so happens, and you well know it that I love liver and onions. Especially the onions part. With mashed potatoes and dark gravy. Now I'm hungry." Standing up, reaching for her ever-present cane, she asked if her mom was coming with them. "I don't mind the company, Gilda Jane, but you will be eating where I want. Not that you have terrible tastes in things, but I want comfort food, not something that costs the world, and I have to stop someplace on the way home to get something more substantial in my belly."

"I was going to suggest the new place called Fling down the street from here." Grandma was already shaking her head, no. "All right. We can go with you. But please, when you order, don't ask for a coloring book for me. I never get enough colors to finish the pictures."

This time, it was Taylor who rolled her eyes. Her mother, she didn't believe, had ever grown up. She knew that it had to have been especially hard on her, losing her husband when they'd only just started out in life, but she didn't know if her mom had always been this way. She didn't know her father other than the stories that they'd tell her. He'd been gone before she'd been able to form any kind of lasting connection with him.

Taylor drove her and Grandma to the restaurant. Mom was taking her own car in the event that she didn't care for anything on the menu. She didn't care one way or the other, but she had a feeling that her grandma had called her this morning for a reason. And they'd not gotten to that as yet.

"I'm sorry, but I can't eat here. They deep fry things, and that's not good for your body. Harriette, you should consider not—" Grandma put up her hand to stop Mom from browbeating her about the food. "I'm just trying to tell you that it's not all that healthy for you."

"Gilda Jane, I'm nearly ninety-nine years old and I don't give a good fig if they deep fry fingers and call them Frenchie fries. I want comfort food, not some kind of fad diet that I didn't eat as a child. Now, I'm going to go have me a meal that I can be too full from but enjoy it enough to suffer from the pangs of it. You can stay or not. I'm having a good meal."

Her mom left them there with a huff. She

actually stomped her foot on the way out, too. Shaking her head, Jeri followed. She wondered if they'd be together much longer.

"I wonder if the two of them are suited." Taylor told her grandma that she was thinking the very same thing. "I don't know what gets into her sometimes. I wonder now what my grandson saw in her. But I can forgive her almost anything because I have you at my side. Let's have the buffet, darling. I really do want something that will stick to my ribs."

Grandma really didn't eat that much, certainly not enough that it cost them to get the buffet. But she was happy, and that's all she cared about. When she ate the last of her slice of chocolate silk pie, she looked at her. Bracing herself, she leaned back to listen to what she had to say.

"I'm old." That, for some reason, made her laugh. "I don't believe that's the least bit funny young lady. Why would you laugh at me?"

"Grandma, you've been old since I was a child. But it never seemed to stop you before. What's really going on? Did a doctor tell you something that will make me have to hunt him down and murder him?" Grandma pulled out her hankie and wiped at her cheeks. "I'm sorry,

Grandma. Tell me what he said to you if that's what is going on."

For a few minutes, they didn't say anything. Their teas were refilled, and Grandma asked for some hot tea as well. Taylor didn't drink tea in any form, but she did have a refill of her water. After what seemed like to her a very long time, she turned to look at her.

"You remember that young man that you told me about when you were in high school? Did you know that he went on to get his law degree?" Taylor asked her if she meant Hudson Tucker. "Yes, that's him. He married a lovely woman, and she's an attorney too. I've contacted him for some changes in my will. Actually, it's a big undertaking, and I'm not looking forward to it. I've not done a revision to it since my grandson passed. I need to update a few things."

"All right. Is there a reason for this to be done now?" She told her what she'd told her mother, that she was ninety-nine. "Grandma, I don't know if you believe this or not, but you have a lot to live for. Also, you don't act like anyone near your age but as if you were fifty years younger."

"You don't need to butter me up, child. I'm leaving everything to you." She told her grandma no. "What do you mean, no? I can do what I want, and you'll do what I tell you to. I'm leaving it to you so that you can make sure that my wishes are finished. There are a great many places that I'd like to make sure they get what they deserve."

"That sounds like you're telling me one thing but it's not exactly what you're meaning. What do you mean, get what they deserve?" Grandma told her that she was much too smart for her own good. "You've said that to me before. I still don't understand it any more than when I was a child."

"You always were so stable. I do believe that the only reason that your mother is still around is because you switched places with her and became the mother to her. Even at the age of eight, you were able to keep a roof over your heads as well as food in the pantry." Taylor asked her to get to the point. Please. "All right. I'm a very wealthy woman. I have invested well and I've done very well by saving my money for a rainy day. I want you to make sure that a couple of businesses that I have invested in, deadbeat places are going to get what they deserve by suing them. I can't. I just don't want the stress. But you're smart and mean when it comes to standing up for justice."

"I can do that for you. It would be my

pleasure. But I don't understand that it's something that you think needs to be—Grandma, I can't lose you. If you know something, please tell me." She told her again her age. "And as I have pointed out to you several times, you aren't that old in your mind and body. Tell me."

"I'm not going to lie to you, so you'd better be girthing up your loins, child. I have cancer. I know that I've had a long life and a good one, too. But I don't have it in me to fight this disease. I'm refusing chemo. I don't want to linger around sucking the life out of you while you make me try and hang onto life a little longer. I want to go just the way that I lived my life. With my hair on my head and my body not so shot up full of chemicals, that will more than likely have my roses that you're going to plant on my grave glow in the dark. I'll be moving back home from the retirement center. I want the comforts of home around me."

It hurt Taylor to her very core that she was going to lose her grandma. She'd been her rock since she could remember. Losing her and not being able to talk to her every day, she thought that she might well curl up in a ball and die along with her. Then she put her hand over hers, and she looked at the frail hand that used to stroke her as a child when she needed comfort.

"All right. I can...I don't want to lose you, but I understand. I don't have to like it either, but I really do understand." Grandma stood up, and she did as well. Trying to follow her to the cash register, Grandma paid and was out the door before she could gather her own things up. When she got out of the restaurant, she had to think where she'd parked her car and found her grandma there waiting for her. "Have I done something wrong?"

"Not at all. Please, let's just go to that park we used to go to when you were younger." Nodding, she got into the car after unlocking it. Grandma situated herself and buckled in. They were on their way to Glidden Park in just a short few minutes.

They didn't get out of the car, it was too crowded with children running around at the park. Also, she thought it was just a little too chilly for them to be just sitting around talking. Turning to her grandma after turning the car off, she asked her to explain.

"I knew that you'd accept what I was saying. I also know that it hurt you to do that. I love you, Taylor. I couldn't have loved you more for that. But it's been difficult for me too...you understand, don't you? Why I don't want to have those nasty treatments." She told her that she did, but it didn't hurt her any less. "Good. I'd like to think that you're going to miss me, even if it's just a little bit."

They both laughed, they both knowing that it was going to shatter her to lose her after all this time. As they sat there, admiring the beautiful fall afternoon, Grandma started telling her about her life with her late husband. Grandpa Charles. Another family member that she didn't remember.

"My Charlie was full of adventure. He was such a good man and a sap as well." She signed heavily. "There were times in our life that I despaired of us having a roof over our heads. But he always knew what to do when the time was right. Buying and selling things, even things that he'd pick up at garage sales and things like that. I so wish he could have known you. You're so much like him that it's scary at times."

"Thank you." She nodded, and Taylor waited for her to say more. When she didn't, Taylor decided to talk to her about Hudson. "Why him? I mean, you have to know a great many other attorneys that would jump at the chance to help you out with your will?"

"That's precisely it. He wouldn't jump at the chance. He'd watch the others fumble through what I wanted and wait until they messed things up so much that he'd have to step in and take over. He and his wife have a lovely family now and I do believe you've heard of the foundation that he is a part of. Tucker Charities."

"Yes. They're helping me get some land to put the distribution center for the companies that I own put in his town. That charity is a big deal, did you know that? Of course, you did." Smiling, she reached for Grandma's hand and held it. "I could finance it myself, but I want the people in the town to have jobs. One of the...I don't remember her name right now but she got in contact with my office begging for an interview. She said that she had a lot of people out of work who would do just about anything to have a steady paycheck. I have a meeting with her tomorrow."

"Good girl. You take them on." Grandma yawned. "I'm so full that I need a good long nap. I'm not saying the forever kind. I still have a little more juice in my old body. But I'm meeting with Hudson this evening to get things squared away with my will. Thank you, Taylor. I knew that I could depend on you."

After dropping off her grandma, Taylor made her way home. She didn't have a house but a condo that she had hated since the moment that she moved in, more than likely the reason that she didn't have any furniture in the place, not even a table with chairs. And it had been eleven years since she'd purchased hers and the rest of the condos in the subdivision where she lived.

Lying down herself, she decided that she needed a nap as well. All those carbs were catching up to her. As soon as she put her head on her pillow, she was out, not even bothering to turn off any of the lights in her room.

~*~

Jack had made sure that after having dinner together, Mrs. Murphy and his brother Hudson weren't disturbed. He'd only just opened up the private area where parties could be held in the restaurant, and he was glad that Hudson had asked to use it. It made him feel like he was liking Jack's.

When Ivy came into the restaurant, he smiled, taking his nephews in his arms for a hug. Archie said he was too old for hugs, so his sister, Lisa, shoved him out of her way and hugged him too. She asked him why he always hugged her last.

"Because, my dear, you give the best hugs." She hugged him again. "I take it you're here for dinner? I have a lot of things on the menu that I hope are kid friendly. You wouldn't want to try a few of them out for me, would you?"

"I would love to, but…oh, the heck with it. Homework can wait until later. Yes, we'd love to have dinner. But don't go out of your way for us to have food. The kids will eat just about anything." He told her that he had brussel sprouts and steak tar-tar for them. "I'll have you know that they all eat brussel sprouts."

"No, we don't. We have to eat them. We don't like them." He kissed Lisa on the head before seating them. He had been going to have lunch, too, since it was after the lunch crowd and had the waitstaff bring him a burger and fries. It wasn't on the menu yet; he'd been playing around with different buns, but he thought that he'd had it right.

"I'm batting a thousand with the kids' menu, I think." The kids had wandered off to sit in another booth. He knew that they'd not run around and be heathens, as Grannie used to call kids but sit quietly and color. "I got the coloring pages printed up just yesterday. Shawn did a wonderful job on it. Instead of just being something that older kids would like, she made it something that everyone loved. So tell me, what's wrong? You didn't just come in here to have lunch. I know you better than that, sister dear."

"I'm pregnant again. I'm thrilled, don't get me wrong, but I'm also enjoying getting out in the world too." He didn't understand and told her that. "I'll have to stop working. We'd only just figured out that I was going to be the one working. I enjoyed it so much that Hudson would stay at home and only take things that interested him. Now this."

"I don't see why that has to change. I mean, I don't have children, nor have I ever had a baby, but I don't understand why you think you'd enjoy your job any less than you do after the baby is born." She cried a little before he could figure things out. "Oh honey, don't cry. Hudson will murder me if he thinks that I caused those tears."

"What about after the baby is born?" He shrugged, still clueless about what she was upset about. "I mean, Hudson won't be able to nurse the baby. It'll all be on me to be there for that."

"I see. I want to tell you something. This might have just come about, but I hear they have this thing called formula. Someone feeds it to the baby when you're not at home." She smacked his hand. "Also, I doubt very much that anyone would care as much as Hudson will that you don't want to be stuck at home nursing a baby all the time. I don't know how long that takes. Again, I can't have children, but it's surely not an all-day event, right?"

"A few hours a day." He nodded, then asked her if she could, and he assured her that he didn't know. Couldn't she just put it in a bottle for the baby or have Hudson bring it in to her. "When did you become so brilliant with matters of a child, Jack? Surely, you've not been hiding a child away from us."

"Nope. I've always been brilliant. I just don't let it out there as much as the others do." She smacked him again but with laughter. "I don't know what I said that had you smiling but I'll do whatever you need to make it so that you do it all the time. I'm sure that my brother will be thrilled too to have to feed the baby on his own. I've never seen a man so devoted to being a stay-at-home dad. Yesterday, he told me he was taking the kids to swim class. He looked to me like he'd invented the project."

"He and the kids are planning a garden for next year. They were out there a couple of days ago digging in the dirt so that they could plant peas. Peas, of all things. While home, back in Ohio, we barely had time to grocery shop, much less put a garden in. But here, with all the things that we've gotten, not only can we grow our own things, but there isn't as much pressure to help make ends meet that way. I don't know what we would have done if Grannie hadn't had us over for dinner a few times a week. I think that was all that kept us from going under." He told her that was why he had lived in the big house. It afforded him the ability to eat and have gas money. "And now, look how far we've come thanks to Denver. All he did was get out and talk to a few people and we're all living well and happy. And Jack, I'm very happy."

"So am I. Very much so. And you're so right. All this is due to Denver. And him being Leap Leader has made a difference in your lives as well. Hudson just didn't like it, did he?" She said that he stressed about it all the time. "I can see him doing that. Stressing when there was no reason for it. However, I also know that he is more relaxed than I've ever seen him since he's given it up, too."

"Denver is doing a good job. And the fact that he had Ronan and Brook in his corner helped a great deal. I don't think that he'll have any trouble once they start pulling away more. Or not. Pulling away, I mean. They seem to be as much a part of our family as anyone else who was born to the Tuckers. Do you miss them?"

Caught off guard by the question, Jack asked her if she meant their parents. Nodding, he had to think about it. It was something that he'd never given a great deal of thought about before.

"I don't think that I can give you an answer to that without sounding like a jackass. But you can't really miss something that you've never had before. They were never really a part of our lives. By the time I realized that they weren't coming back, I think that I'd only spent a few years with them with any sort of awareness. I do remember times, but nothing that I could tell you a date on, like her and Dad being selfish about dinner. They'd horde up the meat, usually steak, while we'd have a bread sandwich. You know what that is, don't you? A slice of bread between two more slices. We had those a great deal until I started making our meals. I believe that's where I got my knack for cooking, being desperate for a real meal. After they left? I don't know that it was a lot better but at least there was food on the table all the time."

"Hudson would tell me such horrible things

about his parents and what they did to you guys. Just dropping you all off at your grandmother's was just something that he realized was the best parenting thing they ever did for you." Jack agreed. "I so love your family, Jack. Hudson tells me all the time that they're my family as well, but I can't help but be thankful for the lot of you living where you had. I don't think that they would have been as nice as your grandparents were about me being his mate."

"Because of you being human, you mean." She nodded. "I hate to say this, but he might be right. They were so superior to anyone around them even though they didn't have a pot to piss in, so the saying goes.

A woman came into the restaurant just as they were getting ready to close up for the day. He only did lunches through the week until he could get used to having people around, and so far, everyone was loving it. But the woman only stopped to speak to Beatrice, one of the staff and led her to the room where Hudson was working with Mrs. Murphy. Once the door closed behind them, Ivy said that she was ready to go. That having this time with him had given her a better outlook on life.

After she left, he went into the kitchen to make sure that things were turned off and cleaned up. He had a good crew, he realized once again and he was going to have to do something for them and all their hard work. Leaving a kettle on the stove on simmer, he made sure that there were cups and other things that they might need before they were finished up. He looked up just as a woman, the one from earlier, came into the room.

"Grandma sent me in here to get some tea and cookies. She called them scones, but I don't think that is really what she...she has a great deal of money, did you know that?" She looked stressed, so he didn't move toward her, afraid that she'd maybe freak out more. "A great deal of it... can I take the tea into them? Your brother, you look like him. He said that you could go after this, and he'd make sure things were put back when he was finished. She's leaving it all to me so that I'll take care of...it's a great deal of money."

"You said that. Twice now. Are you all right?" She nodded, then shook her head. "Yeah, I'm getting that feeling from you as well. Why don't you have a seat and I'll take this into them. Give yourself a little time before you go back in there."

She sat down. Like she'd been just waiting for someone to tell her that's what she needed to do. When he asked her again, she looked up at him with glazed eyes before nodding and then shaking her head again.

"Yeah, all right then. You stay here, and I'll be back. If it's all right with you, I won't mention that you're having a stress attack. Unless you want me to." She told him not to mention it. "Okay. Well, I'll be back. Did you want some tea? Something to eat? I have leftover salad fixings that I can make up for you."

"No. I think I'm all right now." He nodded, still not sure. "I am. I promise you. I was just shocked, well, that's an understatement. Grandma said she was…you know what? I'm fine. I'll take in the tea stuff and help with serving it. Just the initial shock of learning that she had billions of dollars startled me, I suppose you could say."

He didn't say anything but kept an eye on her as she loaded up one of the new smaller trays that he'd gotten the other day. When she was gone, Jack let out a breath that he'd been holding and sat down himself. Christ, she had made him stressed, and he didn't even know who she was.

After locking up, he headed home. He'd not

even been close to the woman, but she was all he could think about. Deciding to take a shower, he stripped down and thought about what he was going to wear while around the house. When the exact set of clothing, an old t-shirt and jersey shorts, appeared on him, he leaped back. Hitting his head on the doorframe and knocking himself out. His last thoughts were that he'd met his mate and hadn't even realized that.

Chapter 1

Jack was still sitting in his kitchen when the sun was coming up the next morning. If asked, he couldn't have for the life of him said a single thing that he'd been thinking about. Or, for that matter, if he'd thought of anything at all. His mind was full of fluff right now, and he didn't know what to do about it. He'd met his mate. And other than the fact that she was going to inherit a great deal of money—billions from her grandmother, he didn't know another thing about her.

She'd said billions. He was sure of that. While he had money, a great deal of it too, he thought, he didn't have anywhere near the billion-dollar mark and was afraid of what that might mean for him. Billions of dollars was something like the Fosters had. Not some little lion that—well, he was a full-grown man, but a billion was well beyond more than he would have thought that he'd get in his lifetime.

He needed to figure out where to find her.

Or, at the very least, her name. When he thought about it, he'd not even known the name of the woman that his brother was meeting with last night in his restaurant. Not that it would help him overly much if she was her grandmother on her mother's side. Then there was the—standing up, he decided to get his ass in gear before he got himself in trouble. With whom he didn't know, but he wasn't going to mess things up before he even got to meet the woman.

It took him an hour to get in touch with Hudson. Being a stay-at-home dad, he didn't answer the phone very often and he was afraid to bother him with their link in the event he was in the middle of something with the kids. Jack thought for sure that he was making too much of this, but he didn't know what else to do.

"I think that Georgie has a meeting with her today sometime. Her name is Taylor. Last night, when I met her, I could have sworn that the two women were mother and daughter; they acted that close, but they're actually great-grandmother to great-granddaughter. Why did you want to know?" Since he knew that he'd find out sooner or later, he told him what had happened last night when he met the girl. "Mate? You're kidding. I hate to say this to you, Jack, but she's going to eat you alive. She's hard and brash. But she loves her grandmother."

"Gee, thanks. When she came into the kitchen, I didn't realize it as I never got close to her in the kitchen until I got home and took a shower, and my clothing just appeared. That's a sure sign, isn't it? She's the only stranger I met yesterday who would have had me getting that sort of magic where I can change. Do you know where she lives?" He was babbling and making disjointed statements that made him sound stupid, something else he'd never done before meeting his mate.

"Actually, I do. She lives in the same condo complex that you live in. But she won't be there. Her grannie asked her to move in with her for a few days so that she could go over some contracts. Your mate is wealthy already, but when her grannie passes, she'll be right up there with Ronan and his family." He said he didn't care about that but wanted to know why he thought that she would eat him alive. "I don't know, Jack. You're sort of timid. Not a sap but just someone that has to be pushed into things."

"I'm just cautious." His brother laughed.

"Well, laugh it up, big brother. I know that I'm going to be better at meeting my mate than the rest of you were. Especially you. Didn't you and Ivy fight right up until you were married? And I remember some harsh words before your oldest was born, too."

"That's when things smoothed out. We are both competitive people, and I realized that once she started taking on cases, she was smarter than me, too. I don't remember the last time we had a spat, to be honest. I love Ivy with all that I am." He told him that it shows, too. "I want you to be as happy as we all are, Jack, so keep that in mind when things get heated. She's smart too, don't forget that."

After talking to his brother, he made his way over to the condo that his brother told him that she lived in. He'd been right. The place was in the same subdivision he lived in, yet there was no one home. Jack made his way to the address that he'd been given him for her great-grandmother. Returning to get his car, he was slightly nervous about finding the house and where the address was. It was in the posh end of town.

As he drove down the tree-lined street after turning on the one that he needed, all he could think about was how big the houses were. Counting down the house numbers, he just knew that the house that he was looking for was going to be not only the biggest one on the street but also the most beautiful.

Pulling into the gated drive had him asking for permission to enter to talk to Taylor. The man at the gate said he'd have to check but would get back with him. It seemed like hours before he came back and told him where to go. He wished he'd have changed into a suit, then decided that he was fine, like he was in jeans and a nice shirt and tie. As soon as he got out of the car, he was greeted by a gardener who told him where Miss Taylor was.

He watched her pulling carrots out of a long row of similar-looking greens. Her feet were bare, and she had on the ugliest straw hat he'd ever seen. But it suited her as did her working in the garden. Getting her attention, she pulled off her gloves and stuck them into her basket, overflowing with fresh fall vegetables. He introduced himself to her and reminded her that she'd seen him last night.

"I'm Taylor Murphy. You must be Hudson's brother. That's right, I remember now, I met you last night." He said that she had. "I was slightly freaked out but getting a better handle on things today." He followed her to the back of the house to the door. "Mrs. James, she's our cook, is going to have a pot roast tonight, and the thought of fresh carrots and potatoes with it made my mouth water. She's making zucchini bread too." She looked at him. "I'm having a hard morning so far. I'm sorry to babble. My grandma is dying, and I hate the thought of losing her."

He held her while she cried. Every part of him wanted to figure out how to make her grannie better because of the sobs that were tearing at his heart. When he seemed to have gathered herself up, she pulled away and started washing off the vegetables in the basket and talking about the weather. There were still breaks in her voice, but she didn't seem to need him anymore.

"It's supposed to be warmer tomorrow, but I couldn't wait to get out here. I could spend my entire day outside and never get all the things done that need to be done. It's wonderful too that the house is self-efficient in that it doesn't buy fruits and vegetables unless we run out. Our meat as well comes from a ranch that we have in another county. And in all the years that I've been here, that's never happened. The household also has another ranch that raises milking cows and goats for our cheese and other dairy products. I love living here more than I do anyplace else in the world." She led him to the large garden in the back of the house. It took up an entire acre of land that looked like something his own grannie would have envied. "There are trees too that give us plenty to use as well as bushes of other kinds of fruit. The entire house is heated by the wood, too, that we cut down when it's necessary. I love this place so very much."

She took him to the several barns and to the other plots of gardens that had people working in them. There were long lines of flowers, fresh for the house she told him so that summer was in all the time. After they had toured the most beautiful deck that he'd ever seen, he wanted to beg to work there just so he'd have access to all the things that she'd shown him around the house. It must have taken years to get them to this point, and he wished that he'd been a part of it from the beginning.

"I didn't catch your name." He told her his name and shook her hand, getting a shock of something rolling between the two of them. "I'm sorry to have taken up all your time this morning. I needed it, and I can't thank you enough for letting me go on and on. Are you here to see my grandmother? I think she was on the phone when I last saw her."

"It was my pleasure. I heard that you were to have a meeting with my sister-in-law today. I hope that I didn't take up your time in that." She said that she was going to have lunch with them, he could too if he wished. "I don't want to intrude. I only came out to…I didn't touch you yesterday, so I didn't know until I got home. Then, when it happened, like a fool, I sat around my place thinking of nothing but the fact that you were her. After talking with Hudson, I needed to find out—"

"I'm confused. What happened to you?" He nodded, trying his best to figure out a way to tell her when he heard someone calling out her name. "I have to go in. Will you come in and explain to me what you meant?"

"I'm your mate." She didn't seem to want any more explanation, so when she put up her hand, he didn't say anything more. Following her to the back deck again, she asked him to talk to her after her meeting with Georgie was over. He didn't know how that was going to work since Georgie would know as soon as she saw him. There were no secrets when it came to finding mates, he understood.

Georgie seemed glad to see him. Since he was sure that either she'd figured out what Taylor was to him or Hudson had told her, she didn't say a word about them being mates. Lunch wasn't ready, so the four of them, including Mrs. Murphy, joined them in the big office, and he watched as the two younger women got down to business. After about another hour, they were called to eat.

There was zucchini bread to go with the warmed butter and vegetable soup that was a part of the basket full of things he'd watched Taylor gather. Also, much to his delight, there were fresh sliced apples with homemade caramel in a cup to dip the apples into.

When Mrs. Murphy was finished with lunch, she asked him to join her in her gardens. He didn't want to disappoint her, so he was ready to go look at them again. This time with her. But it wasn't the vegetable garden that he'd already seen but the orchards as well as her flower gardens.

"We grow them for the house. There are always fresh flowers in the house throughout the year. I so love that they put them in the front hall so that a person can see them first thing. They also use some of the edible ones for salad and garnish." She picked him one and handed it to him. "These are my favorite. They have a delicate taste that I so enjoy and the flowers are the most beautiful yellow in the early spring."

"It tastes like cucumber." After his excitement with the first bloom, she handed him more and had him guess the flavor. "I think that this was in our soup too. Next time, I won't be so quick to push them to the side, thinking that they're just there for show."

"Do you believe there will be a next time?" Her voice was so low that he might not have heard it if he'd been human. "I'm dying, young man. And if I know my shifter lore correctly, you and my granddaughter are mates, am I right?"

"Yes, you're right. I told her when I first got here and then she seemed to not want to talk about it." She told him how she had a great deal going on at the moment, but she was still thinking about what he was to her. "I don't know her well enough to know that. She's very intense, isn't she?"

"As I said, she has a great deal going on. I just told her the other day that I'm probably not going to make it to my hundredth birthday, and she's dealing with all the businesses I'm going to leave her in charge of. Then there is her mother." He asked about the mother. "I've asked Taylor to live with me in my final months, and she has agreed. I'm glad now that she'll have you here with her when I pass. But her mom is none too happy with the fact that I won't allow her to be here, too. I love Gilda Jane, but she'll drive me batty with her flighty ways, and that won't do any good to anyone while at this point of my life."

"I've never met her, I don't think." Harriette, as she asked him to call her, assured him that he'd remember her if he had. "Do you think that she'll cause trouble after you're gone? And if so, what sort of trouble so that I can keep track of her."

"I don't know that Gilda Jane has enough sense to cause trouble. But that's what will drive me and her daughter insane. She'll be sticking her nose into business that doesn't concern her. Whatever it will be, Gilda Jane will think that she has the best advice on things and will be like a dog with a bone in telling you how you're doing things wrong. And she treats me as if I'm a doddering old woman who needs to be yelled at to be able to hear her. Oh, she just frustrates me to no end. And if not for Taylor, I would have turned her out long ago." When she burst into tears, he sat down beside her and held her in his arms. She was so upset and crying so hard he was tempted to find

Gilda Jane and beat the snot out of her for making this wonderful woman so heart brokenly upset.

When she calmed down, he continued to hold her. Given the chance to look around he couldn't believe the colors and the vegetation that was surrounding him. It was enough to make his own beast calm a bit, and more than that, he felt as if he was at peace with the world here.

"You must think me to be an old fool." He smiled and told her that he didn't believe that she was either. "Thank you for that. I've had a rough few days myself, as a matter of fact. The doctor is telling me that I'm going to suffer in the end without chemicals in my body. I told my granddaughter that I wanted to leave this world just the way I came into it. With my body without chemicals and my hair on top of my head." He laughed. It just struck him as funny that she was so furious about her needs.

While she gathered herself together, he wandered not far from where she was sitting. There was plenty for him to see, and it didn't take him long to see that other things were growing in the garden. For so late in the summer or early fall, there were lots of pumpkins growing between the roses. Zucchini was growing along and over the fence that he was sure was meant to keep the deer out. He noticed, too, that fruits were growing along the back fence that looked to him to be blueberries. He didn't know they would grow this late in the year.

"You've made me feel better, young Jack." Jack told Harriette that it was his pleasure to be there with her when she needed it. "I didn't realize that I had until I started sobbing like a small child. Do forgive me. I do feel much better. I guess it's true that you need a stranger to cry on their shoulders once in a while."

"You have me for so long as you wish." He heard the door open and looked up to see Georgie and Taylor coming toward them. When Taylor asked her grandma why she'd been upset, she glared at him. "I didn't do anything but comfort her when she needed it. I swear to you —"

"Don't get your panties in a twist, Taylor. He was there for me when I got a bit overwhelmed." Nodding, Taylor apologized to him. "He's a good man to have in your corner. I was just telling him about your mother, too. And how she wants to come here. It just overcame me a bit, and he was there for me."

"You didn't change your mind about her,

did you?" Shaking her head no, she said that he'd not do that but just gave her a shoulder to cry on for a bit. "Well, thank you for that. Georgie and I have come to an agreement. She's going to help me bring my distribution center here with good tax cuts as well as all the employees that I need. A win all the way around, I think."

~*~

Taylor didn't want to talk about being his mate. She didn't want to talk to anyone at the moment. Her head was stuffed full of things that she needed to take care of and having him around all the time was making her crazy. Well, not really. He'd been a gentleman, and it seemed like he was a good balm for her grandmother, too. While waiting for dinner to be ready, the three of them met in the living room to talk.

"I was just telling your grandmother what I wouldn't give to have a garden like you guys do here. I could not only supply my home with food, but the restaurant would benefit from it as well. I could make my menu according to what was in season. I've not lived here long enough to know what's in season or not year-round, but it would be fun to have fresh throughout." She rattled off some of the things that she knew were in season right now. "I noticed that you had pumpkins. The things that my grandma could do with just one of them used to amaze you. Pumpkin soup, my favorite, would be a real treat with homemade bread and pumpkin log or pie for dessert."

"You came here for what?" He told her, much more politely than she'd spoken to him, that he'd come to tell her that they were mates. "And you think that because we are, you can come into this house and demand things that don't belong to you."

"Taylor Ann Murphy. What is the matter with you? This is my house and my guest, and you'll treat him with the same respect that you would anyone else." Harriette told Jack how sorry she was and then glared at her. "He's been nothing but a nice man to the two of us and a comfort to me."

"I'm sorry. I'm...I've been out of sorts for the last week." Jack told her that he understood and was sorry that he caused her some more stress. "I'm sure that Grandma told you that she's dying. It's taken all I have not to be sitting in a corner sucking my thumb."

"I don't know what I'd do if my grannie were to be in the same situation. However, she's a lion, so I don't expect her to be able to get cancer. That's a terrible thing for anyone to have." Her grandma agreed. Taylor looked away, her eyes filling with tears again. "Tell me about the project that you're going to be doing with Georgie and the foundation. She said if it worked out, there would be more jobs in the area." She didn't want to tell him anything. Her heart was like that of late, just shutting down for hours at a time so that she didn't have to think or be hurt anymore. "Taylor?"

"It's going to create over five hundred jobs for the area, both before the building is put up and after." After a few seconds she started telling them both what was going to go on and what kind of sales and such she thought that she'd be getting. "We'll have a distribution center here that will also sell damaged items to the employees at a great discount. As well as benefits, each person will have insurance if they wish to get it as well as the foundation will provide transportation for the first six months. We both figured that it would take that long for a person to be able to save up for a car or something along those lines. But they'll continue to help them so long as they're showing an effort."

She found it comforting to talk to Grandma

and Jack. Leaning back in the chair she was in, Taylor could feel her back begin to relax as well as her entire body. Before she knew it, someone was gently shaking her awake. It took her several seconds to realize that it was Jack and that her grandma had gone on ahead of them.

"I almost didn't want to wake you. You looked so relaxed and comfortable." Sitting up, with his help, he asked her to take her time so that she'd not get too dizzy standing. She was feeling slightly wobbly and held onto his hand while she let her legs get under her again. It was then that she noticed his scent.

It wasn't cologne. Not anything that she'd ever smelled before, anyway. But he smelled good, great even. Burying her nose into the crook of his neck, she inhaled deeply and heard his moan. Her own reaction made her body feel less settled and more carnal.

Like she needed him to strip her down and take her right there on the floor. If he had not pulled her closer, Taylor was sure that she would have done just that to him. When he pulled back, it was everything that she could do not to beg him to take her. When she looked at him, thinking that there would be humor in his eyes, she was startled to see lust from him.

His eyes were dark brown, so dark that they looked black. His hair was a tawny brown color that seemed to have come alive with her touching him. Taylor didn't have any choice but to touch him, drag her fingers from the top of his head to his ears where she wanted to be in the worst sort of way.

"Taylor." His voice was husky. Like dark chocolate to her with bits of spice to make her want even more from him. "If you keep looking at me like that, I'm going to drag you to the floor and have my way with you."

"Promise?" Shivering when he stepped back, she had to reach for him when she had a sudden dizzy spell again. When he took another step back, she realized that they weren't alone in the room. Baker, her grandmother's butler, cleared his throat, not for the first time she'd bet, and took the tea trolley out of the room with him. She was both defensive and embarrassed. Before she could snap at Jack, which she knew she was going to do, he kissed her on her mouth and guided her to the dining room. As she was seated, all she could think about was how wanton she'd just acted to a near stranger.

The conversation went on around her. She knew that her grandmother was telling him about her, but for the life of her she couldn't engage in the conversation once. Even when looked at by them both, her mind couldn't have picked up on the conversation if her life depended on it. Instead, she ate her soup and tried her best to pay attention to the things going on around her.

"Do you have a place in mind where your plant is going to go?" She looked at Jack, feeling she should know who he was, but her mind again had gone off the rails. "Did Georgie give you an idea where you were going to be setting up?"

"There are several hundred acres that are just out of town near a smaller town. We can start building almost as soon as the paperwork it signed by the partners of Tucker Charities." She felt good about having that much information at her fingertips. Smiling, she told him that the place would be a good place for her to be able to expand, too. "I've not been able to expand in the other places I've set up with. I'm excited that in ten years, I'll be able to close down one of the smaller older centers and redo it to be more efficient and more up-to-date. It's what they all need, but I'm only able to do it because of the deal that I've made here."

They talked about the expansion as well as the other things that she'd spoken to Georgie about. She also told Jack that she thought that Georgie should be in charge of getting more jobs around the area.

"I think that they've given her that title. She's been around here longer than we have, and I think she has a better idea of what's going on than we do." She thought that it was great that he was willing to admit that he didn't know much more than a person that had—"You're frowning again. What is it that I've done, and I'll fix it?"

"Nothing. I'm still processing." He nodded and put his hand over hers. The simple contact of his skin against hers had her calming not just her thoughts but also her heart, too. "I'm not sure what to think about you being my mate. It's a lot to take in."

"For both of us." She'd not thought of how this would be to him. He'd been around mates in his family before, and she'd not. Taylor couldn't even remember the last time she'd been on a date. When he laughed, she looked at him, ready to do battle. "I don't know what you're thinking, but if you ask me, I'll give you the best answer that I can. I won't — not that I would, but I can't lie to you about anything. I'll never cheat on you. You alone hold my heart and soul. You will own my heart forever, Taylor. No matter what, I belong to you."

"I don't know what to think about that." He told her that he could understand that as well. It was different for her, too. "Are you always going to be so nice to me?"

He laughed. It looked as if it had startled him as well, the way that it seemed to burst from his mouth. There was humor in his face and eyes, and his body relaxed a bit more. When she looked around, she realized that the two of them were the only ones in the room. Also, their plates had been cleared away, and a bottle of water was set before her.

"Your grandmother said that she was going to go to bed. She did mention that she felt better than she had in a while, and I'm happy for that." She asked him if he'd done any magic on her. "I don't know that I did or didn't. I know nothing more than that. I believe that we both have more magic. At least you will have something more than me, but I don't know what. I can change my clothing with a thought. I'm sure that you can do that as well. Whatever else you got, I haven't any idea. I guess we'll have to wait and see."

They made their way to the living room again and sat on the couch together. Not close enough for them to touch but not too much distance between them. As they were running out of things to say, she laid her head back and closed her eyes. It was the most wonderful feeling knowing that she didn't have to go it alone in her life.

Waking up, she was sad to find herself alone on the couch. She didn't know why but that was the first feeling that she'd had. There was one of the blankets that was forever on the couch over her, and she snuggled down into it. That was when she noticed that there was an envelope on the table across from her.

"Taylor, I didn't want to wake you, so I let you sleep. I've gone home and will call you later. No, that won't work. I don't know your number." His was penciled in at the end of the note. "Have a wonderful day, and I'll talk to you more tomorrow. I enjoyed spending time with you and hope to do it more as we get to know one another." Then it was signed "Love, Jack."

Chapter 2

Gilda Jane was sitting in her kitchen when she realized that she needed to talk to her daughter. It wasn't fair of her to just leave her to her own devices. Taylor had always made sure that things were taken care of for her and she didn't understand why things were suddenly different. Jeri came out of the bedroom that they shared with her luggage. That was another thing that she needed to blame on her daughter.

"I'm leaving." Gilda Jane said that she didn't want her to leave now that Taylor wasn't around. "You're not a lesbian, Gilda Jane, and you never will be the way you feel about same-sex people. I understand that it was a fling for you, you and I together, but you're breaking my heart more and more daily, and I don't want to be around when you finally realize what I already know. You aren't a lover of mine. Anyone's either for as much as I can see about you."

"But you must stay with me. My daughter

and Grandmother in law have kicked me to the curb." Which wasn't right at all. She had a lovely place to live at no cost to herself and pretty things all around her when she wanted them because Taylor made sure that she had money to spend. Jeri moved her two pieces of luggage closer to the door. "Please stay with me. I'll fix up the other room for you. I don't want to be alone."

"And I don't want to be alone, but living here with you means that I won't find someone who will love me." Gilda Jane said that she did love her. "No. You liked the idea of trying to love me, I think, to simply shock your family. They didn't seem the least bit surprised, so I'm thinking that they're less predigest than you seem to be."

"That's not fair. I tried." Jeri shook her head and opened the door. "You can even have lovers over if you want. I don't care. I just don't want to be alone anymore."

"Good bye, Gilda. You might have a better chance of finding someone if you let go of your daughter and live your life the way that you want. Not that way that you want your kid to see you." She told her that she didn't understand. "Stop trying to shock your family by doing things that you think they'll have trouble with. Just be yourself."

She didn't know how to be herself. All her life, she'd been told what she should be and that had gotten her married and a child. Then, the only person she'd been trained to take care of had died of a massive stroke, and she was left with a child that she wasn't sure she even wanted either. It wasn't until one day she seemed to wake up and Taylor was taking care of her that she realized that she could learn to be what Taylor wanted. However, that never worked out. Taylor, like Jeri, wanted her to find her own path, and she'd been wandering listlessly since then.

Trying new things and fades had gotten her a name for being flighty. When she would give up, say the diet of eating only healthy, it was just one more thing that she could blame on Taylor—she wouldn't help her get her head on straight, and it left her to wander around like some thoughtless being that had no idea how to live. She didn't even know how to make her bed, run the dishwasher, or, for that matter, do a load of laundry.

Taylor could. And she did when she came by her place to check up on her. Not only could she get her house in order but she helped her fill out her checks for bills and get them off to the post office. Taylor had wanted her to set up online paying, but she couldn't make that work either. Something about having to get on the computer once in a while to make sure that things were being paid would mess her up.

Gilda Jane didn't have credit cards for the same reason. She'd forget there were balances on them and not pay them off at the end of the month. If she wanted anything, she'd have to find either Henrietta or Taylor to go with her to use their credit cards so that she'd have nice things all the time.

Taylor had admitted that she'd made it so that her mom would have to depend on her for everything. And she was sorry for that. Gilda Jane wasn't sorry. It made is so that she would get to see her daughter more often. Of course, even when Taylor had set up things for her like her groceries being brought to her, she would mess up the order just to bring her daughter running. It was why she messed up all the things in her life so that her daughter would come to her and bail her out. It was her thing to see her more often.

Of course, she could get upset with her, too, like last month when she'd ordered a gross of oranges. Gilda Jane knew that was a great many oranges, but for two days, Taylor helped her get out of the order and she loved that like the car that she had too.

She hated to drive. It would make her crazy to have to remember all the rules about it. Where to park and stop. How to find her car when she drove it someplace and parked it. No one would ever know that she had been pretending that she had forgotten her car just so she could be the center of attention for Taylor when she was lonely. Now she was living with Henrietta, and she wasn't allowed to be there too.

Taylor had told her that she needed to learn the businesses that her grandmother was leaving her. Not understanding how it could be that hard to run a business. She'd seen some of the business owners sitting around at their desks all the time when she'd been out and about. She didn't even know what Henrietta did, for that matter. The woman didn't seem to do much of anything anyway. Picking up the phone to call Taylor, she wasn't happy with the way that she answered.

"Mom, I told you that I'm much too busy today to help you. I'll be there on Friday, and I'll bring some lunch, and we'll go over your accounts again." She told her how Jeri had left her, and she didn't want to be alone. Then asked again if she could please move in with her and her grandmother. "No. I don't have the energy to help you and help grandmother as well. You have friends around you there. Go out to lunch with one of them and have some fun."

"They're busy." She didn't know if they were busy or not, but that's what they said when she told them that she was lonely and that she wanted one of them to move in with her. No one wanted to be her friend when she was lonely anymore. "Taylor, I should mean more to you than your grandmother. If she's really dying, which I don't believe for a second, then she should just get it over with so that I can have you all to myself."

"What a terrible thing to say, mother. I can't believe that—why are you being so selfish? Grandmother took care of us after Dad died, and you told me that she made it possible for us to have his insurance money when it was needed." She told her again how lonely she was. "Right now, I don't care how lonely you are. You're being selfish and mean, and I don't have time to be your mother again. Grow up."

When the line went dead, Gilda Jane couldn't believe her ears. "There must have been something wrong with the phone, that's all. There is no way that she'd hang up on me like I'm no one to her. Silly girl. I need her to take care of me like she always did."

Gilda Jane had been talking to herself since she'd been a small child. When she was looking for a husband — her parents were looking for a husband for her, they told her that she would have to stop doing that. And for years, right up until Henry Paul died, she'd not spoken to herself at all but in her mind. Now, if she didn't speak to herself at least three times a day, she couldn't function. It was the way that she got things done. She remembered her mother having a talk with her about her getting married.

"We're too old to keep caring for you, Gilda Jane. You need to find yourself a husband so that he can take care of your needs. And please don't have any children. I don't think that you can handle having someone depend on you as much as a baby will. Just get yourself a man and marry him so that we can go on peacefully in our golden years. It's been too much for us to raise you now that you're in your late twenties." She tried to reason with her mother, telling her that she was happy with the arrangements. "Well, we're not. It's been several lifetimes of caring for your every slightest need. It's time for you to grow up and be on your own."

It didn't happen that way for her. Not only did she find a husband that didn't want to take care of her every need but he didn't want to have to have her around him all the time when he was trying to make a living. She couldn't see why she couldn't go to work with him daily. She had promised him that she'd be quiet and good. But he didn't allow it, so she had to be stuck at home all day. Then, the baby came along.

Gilda didn't know anything about babies. She'd never babysat for one. Never had any sisters or brothers of her own to hang out with. And even though she'd been told that it wasn't Taylor's fault, she demanded things that Gilda Jane couldn't understand why someone else didn't come in and care for them both.

But as Taylor got older, about six years of younger, she began to take care of her, and as her mother was thrilled when there were no more chores or work for her to do to raise a baby. Even after Henry Paul died, Taylor had set aside her grief and had made sure that she was first in everything she did. Even setting up a meeting with her grandmother so that they could have a nice place to live. There were servants there as well that helped. But when Taylor moved out on her own at seventeen, she had to leave as well. Henrietta didn't want her around messing with her plans. Plans that seemed to never cater to her needs but those of her grandmother-in-law.

When her phone rang again, she thought for sure it was Taylor telling her that she was on her way. Instead, it was a sales man that was asking her if she had any property near the ocean. She told him that she did and then asked him if he did.

Thirty minutes later, he'd hung up on her. She couldn't get him to come to her house to visit with her nor would he tell her what sort of house he had. When he did hang up on her, he seemed to be very angry and pissed off. Telling her that she needed to get a life. Mean people didn't understand what it was like to be her. Not even her own family understood how it was to be in her life.

Gilda Jean was going to mess with her grocery order again just to get Taylor to realize how much she needed her. But she told her then that if she did it again, she was going to have to go and buy her own things at the store and then bring them home for herself. That was entirely too much trouble for her and she decided that it wasn't worth having Taylor coming over and being mean to her either. Sitting in the living room, she read the instructions on how to turn on the television and get to the station that she liked. Taylor had even made her instructions on how to turn the volume up and down, too. She supposed that she did love her at times.

She didn't dare make herself some popcorn. The last time she'd done that, she'd burnt up the microwave and had done damage to the rest of the place. Now, all she had were bags of already popped corn that she could enjoy, too. But she was alone and popcorn never tasted as good as it did when she had company.

By evening, she was waiting for her dinner to come to her. It was Wednesday so she'd have pizza for her dinner and her lunch tomorrow. Another thing that Taylor had set up for her so she didn't have to worry about cooking. While she was eating it, sitting at her dining room table for six, it just made her upset that she didn't have anyone to share with. Or even to have a long conversation with someone. She didn't even care if it was the weather they talked about. It would be nice to have—Gilda Jane heard someone down at the pool and decided to find herself a seat with the others and pretend that she was there with their families.

She'd done it before and had been asked to not put herself in a situation of whipping a child that wasn't hers. Well, the kid wouldn't listen to her about the things he was eating and she decided to teach him while he was young. The boy's mother didn't see it that way and had called the police on her when she smacked him on the cheek for talking back to her. Taylor would never have done that, and he wasn't going to get by with it either.

Almost as soon as she was seated, one of the mothers told her that there were plenty of other seats to have. Why did she have to sit between them? Ignoring them for covering her skin up from the terrible sun, she laid back and smiled. They'd get used to her being around soon enough.

"Ms. Murphy?" She must have fallen asleep and looked up at the man towering over her. "Ms. Murphy, my name is Jack Tucker. I've been asked to come and see you by your daughter. She wants me to take you home. You've disrupted the pool party enough."

"I'm not bothering anyone. I was just lonely." He asked her if she'd eaten the cake and ice cream. "Yes. It was there, and I'm right here. I saw no reason why I shouldn't partake of it either.

And I only ate a bit of both. They're bad for you with all the sugars and such in them."

"It's time to go home." She gathered up where stuff with his help. Mostly he was picking things up on his own and handing them to her. "Taylor said that she'd talk to you tomorrow, but you're to stay in the condo without bothering anyone. She said you know what she'll do if you don't behave yourself."

"I'm a grown woman." She thought he said for her to act like it but she wasn't sure. "Well, that's all right, I guess. You'll come and stay with me until Taylor calls, and we'll make a night of it. I'm lonely, you see."

"I'm not staying. I have my own place to stay." She pouted at him, which usually worked on men like him, but he only took her keys from her and opened her door. "You heard what I said to you, didn't you? You're to stay in the house until she talks to you. Otherwise, she said that she'd take you to task."

"I wonder at times if she remembers that I'm her mother." She pouted at Jack again. "Can't you just stay until I go to sleep? I won't bother you, I promise."

All he did was shove her inside the condo,

hand her the keys, and slam the door. She'd never been treated so badly in a long time. Well, she'd tell Taylor what a mean person he was so that he'd be out of a job soon enough. The nerve of some people.

~*~

Henrietta didn't know what to think about her doctor's visit. He had to be making her feel better, but as far as she was concerned, it was a cruel trick. To tell her that her cancer was gone was something that she'd never thought to hear. She'd been given only months to live, and now she was told that she could live out her life forever without cancer. Cancer free. It was two words that she'd never thought to hear.

"You don't seem to be happy to hear that." She told him that she was in shock. "To tell you the truth, Ms. Murphy, I am as well. When you were in here last week, I only gave you about ten weeks to live. Now, it wouldn't surprise me to see you living for a good long time. Congratulations. You've been blessed with—a shifter. You know a shifter, don't you?"

"Yes, Jack Tucker. He's mated to my granddaughter, Taylor." He nodded. "He didn't do anything to me. I mean, the most we've shared it a hug. Nothing more."

"He must love you very much, along with Taylor." She asked him what that meant. "He only needed to touch you to heal you. You mean a great deal to him, or perhaps he wanted you to live for Taylor, but I'd say that he's healed you completely. I'd bet anything that you feel better too. No aches and pains that come with age."

"I do feel better, as a matter of fact. I thought it was, well, I thought it was Jack being in love with Taylor so she'd have someone when I was gone, but you know, I even climbed the stairs to come to your office, and it didn't wind me like it usually does. I feel wonderful." He cautioned her about not doing too much. "No, I won't. I mean, I'm nearly a hundred years old. I don't want to fall now and be hurt." Henrietta stretched out her arms and couldn't believe how much better she felt.

On her way home, she decided that she needed to get something for Jack. Nothing big but something that told him that he'd done something special for her and she wasn't going to forget it. As soon as she pulled into the shopping center lot, she knew just what she was going to give him. Going to the jewelry store, she removed the diamonds that her husband had given her and had them put into a band that would suit Taylor. It would do her heart good to have him marrying her only grandchild with one of the many pieces of jewelry that had been hers. She was also going to give him her husband's band. It was silly of her to wear it on a chain around her neck when someone as special as Jack and Taylor could use them. Right then she decided that she was going to make sure that she gave her all her many jewels now and watch her wear them while she was still around to do so.

She knew as soon as she got home that she needed to take it easy. Running around would still kill her. She wasn't as young as she used to be. Taking a nap before dinner, she was almost too excited to sleep. But exhaustion won out, and she smiled as her body began to relax little by little.

She'd forgotten that they were a couple who were going to go out. They were taking things slowly, and she didn't blame them for that. Jack looked to be so much in love with Taylor that it made her slightly jealous, but she couldn't have been happier for the two of them than she was right now. Just as she was settling down with her own dinner, Gilda Jane called. That woman could put a sour note to about anything wonderful she thought.

"Taylor isn't answering her phone. I wanted to talk to her about that employee she sent over here to take me home." She asked her what his name had been, and Henrietta laughed. "I don't like to be treated like I'm a child."

"Then stop acting like one." Gilda Jane said that he'd said the same thing to her. "Good for him. And you might want to get used to seeing him around. He and Taylor are going to be married soon if I don't miss my bet."

The quiet at the other end of the line should have warned her. Gilda didn't like things going on that she'd not been a part of. Or at least told about it beforehand. When she started screaming, much like a child that she'd accused her of being, Henrietta pulled the phone away from her ear so as not to have any damage done to her. It was like a small child having a tantrum.

"She will not marry anyone. Who will take care of me if she has a husband around all the time? He'll suck her dry, I just know it, and I won't have anyone to take care of me. You'll see. She'll spend all her time around him and there won't be—do you suppose they'll have children? Oh, Henrietta, you can't allow her to do that. I remember how much time a child can suck out of your life. Henry

Paul wanted to take care of her all the time, and I was fine by that, but he up and died and left her to me. I don't want to have to be second or third in line for her to come to my needs."

"You selfish bitch. I never realized until this moment what a selfish person...no, that's not true. I knew that you were selfish, but not to the extent that you've just shown me you could be. I'm glad that she's getting married and I hope that she has children while I'm still around so that I can cuddle them as I did their mother. Why are you like this? With your own daughter?" Henrietta didn't know what she expected her to say, but the next words broke her heart.

"I didn't want to have any children. My parents told me not to have any. But Henry Paul said that he'd take care of them if I had them. Then look what he went and did? He died so that I had to care for the little chit." Feeling the tears as they rolled down her cheeks, she listened to Gilda Jane as she went on about how selfish her grandson had been for having a heart attack and leaving her alone. "If she thinks I'm going to allow this, then she's in for a rude awakening. And I'm going to live with them, too, just to make sure that they don't have children and that Taylor devotes all her time to me. I don't deserve to be left out in the cold any more than I deserve to have her all to myself. Henrietta I demand that you put an end to this right now before I have to tell her how I feel about this. No, I won't have it. I'm not made to be not taken care of. I want what is coming to me as her mother."

"I will do no such thing." She thought about Gilda's parents and finally realized that the rumors that she'd heard all Gilda's life were true. "They forced you to marry, didn't they? To get you out of their home? Isn't that right?"

"They said that they were too old to wait on me all the time. Then they shouldn't have had me is my way of thinking." It made her stomach feel off and she put her hand over it. "They ran off when I got married, and I never could find them. Even when I married like they made me, I didn't love Henry Paul. My parents made me do it, and that's what I did."

Some of the conversations that she'd had with her grandson were coming back to her. How stressed he'd been about having to work so hard and then come home to Gilda wanting things of him. She remembered the day that he told her that he was going to be a father, the fear in his voice along with his excitement. It occurred to her right then that Gilda had killed her grandson as if she'd shot him in the head. The stress of being the working one, taking care of a house, then the child had been just too much for him, and he'd had a massive heart attack at just forty years old. So young, and now she thought that she knew why.

"Did you ever help him out around the house? Take care of the baby when she was born?" Gilda just laughed, manic-like, and said that it was her who needed things done for her and not him. "You murdered him then, didn't you? As surely as I'm standing here talking to you, you killed my grandson because you're—you've been selfish all your life, and because of that, Henry died well before his time."

"Taylor is mine, and she'll do what is good for me and only me. I don't care that she thinks that she'll marry. I won't have it. It's too much of a drain trying to get her to do things for me now so she won't marry. Not so long as I have breath in my body. I won't have it."

Henrietta closed the connection and put her phone on the desk. Her heart was shattered, and she didn't know what she could do about it. As much as she didn't want to tell Taylor and Jack, she knew that they'd have to know what sort of person they'd be dealing with. All this time, all the time since her grandson had died, the clues had been right there for her to look at, and she'd ignored them. Now, her heart was broken.

Picking up the phone, she nearly put it down when Jack answered. Telling him how sorry she was that she'd called him by mistake, he seemed to understand that something was going on. No matter how many times she'd told him that it was all right, she'd talk to them later, he insisted that she tell him what had happened. All she could think about at that moment was that if Gilda got her way, then she'd kill off this young man to get what she wanted in the same way that she'd done to her poor grandson.

They arrived not ten minutes later after hanging up the phone. Sobbing so hard that she could barely speak, she tried her best to tell them both what Gilda had said and had done. Holding onto the two of them, her heart hurting for the words that she was repeating for them, Henrietta told them how sorry she was and that she wished that she'd learned sooner about Gilda. Knowing that she'd killed off her only grandson hurt her in ways that she couldn't explain.

"I'll talk to her." She started to tell Taylor that she didn't want to do that, that she'd just hurt her too when Jack said that he'd take care of her. If she would allow it. "I knew that she was childish and selfish, but I never thought of the extent of her ways. To think that she doesn't care that I'm happy and in love but that I only do what she needs of me. How did I never see this before?"

"She's been that way all her life." Henrietta explained about her parents and how they had moved away right after the wedding. "I never saw it because she'd been that way when I was a child. But lately, I've been getting fed up with her about the little things that she does to get my attention. Stupid things like getting into trouble at the condo. Telling the people there how they should be living their lives around her. She had maid service, and she still manages to fuck things up when I'm not at her beck and call." Taylor looked at her, and she put her hand on her head. Her heart hurt so badly for this child who was born with a mother like Gilda.

"Your father would have spoiled you to no end. But he'd been there for you, too." Henrietta smiled at her but knew that it was a painful one. "I didn't see it. He told me how it was at their home, and I thought for sure that it was just growing pains for Gilda that she'd get better once you were older. But nothing happened. She just kept getting worse and worse."

"I'll make sure that she knows what's going on." She didn't envy Jack any of this but knew that if anyone could deal with Gilda, it would be him. "I'll make sure, too, she knows that she won't be hurting either of you again."

"Your lion might come in handy if you do that." Taylor laughed a little. "Nothing like this was anything I thought was going to happen when I got here. I thought for sure that the doctor had given you less time and you were going to leave me sooner."

"Oh, good heavens, I forgot." She told them everything that the doctor had said and asked Jack if he'd done anything. "I'm not mad, son. I love you—did you just tell me that you love Jack, honey?"

"Yes, I've told him tonight, too, but you're the first to know that we'll be getting married soon, and we don't want any fuss about it." She looked at the two of them and then remembered the rings. "Oh, Grandma, this is more special than I could have hoped for. Thank you so much for thinking of the two of us."

Henrietta decided to go out with them. Leaving all their phones at home, they set out to have a celebration dinner and not talk about Gilda. That was going to be difficult, she knew, but she was going to do her damnest to keep the woman's name out of their fun tonight.

Chapter 3

Jack was ready to close the restaurant down for the day when he got one more order. Next week, they were going to do nights three nights a week and he was both looking forward to it and not. The staff was doing well now and seemed to be catching onto what to do very well, and he loved the rush of lunchtime people coming in to eat at his place. Just as he was reading over the order he'd been given, someone reached out to him. He was surprised that it was Taylor.

"I'm with Bailee. She's the one who told me that I could contact you like this. I think we need to have a long talk about things like this, don't you?" He explained to her, laughing, that they'd been really busy of late. *"I know. I have my phone loaded with messages from my mom. Grandma does as well. How about you?"*

"I didn't check. When I left home this morning, I stopped by the store to get some flowers delivered. I loved the way they seemed to have brightened up your

house when I was there." She said that she needed to talk to him could he spare her a few minutes. *"Yes, I can cook and work at the same time. If not, I'll tell you."*

"Don't tell Grandma, but I think my mom keyed my car some time over the last few hours. I was at a meeting with some of the women in your family, and when I came out to leave, the word 'bitch' was written in scratches on my car. I don't know that it was her for sure but I don't have any trouble with anyone else but her lately." He asked her if she'd called the police. *"I wasn't sure that I wanted to get my mom in trouble, but I'm sure that she's not going to stop with a little vandalism, do you?"*

"No. If you ignore her, she'll think that it's all right with you and ramp up her getting back at you. Best to start off right away involving the police so that when it does get bad, they'll have proof of how she escalated things." She asked him if he thought that she would. *"I don't know, honey. You'd be better off answering that than I would. What do you think that she'll do?"*

"Honestly, I never thought that she'd do this to me. But things have changed for her, too. I have you, and I'm not at home where she can just call for me to come over and do what she wants." Jack asked her if

she was going to move back to the condo now that her grannie wasn't dying. *"I wish I knew to what extent she was still going to be around. Then I'd have a better answer for you. Bailee told me that the only one that would know for sure would be the Foster family. One of them is the grand witch and she would have a better idea as to what sort of magic the two of us have gotten."*

"That would be Parker. She and her husband are the most powerful witch and warlock there has ever been. I'll contact them for you and have her come to meet you." He pulled the steak off the grill and put it onto the plate that he'd been lying other items on as they came off the grill for the order. *"Don't be surprised if she just pops to where you are. Bailee would be used to it, but perhaps not you."*

"She's here." He laughed as she closed the connection. Bailee would be able to keep Parker from scaring Taylor too much and he was glad for her help. After finishing up the order, he began shutting down the grill and the prep table he'd been using. It was nice to have a job that he loved, he knew but he was missing time too in getting to know Taylor and her grandma.

The wedding plans were just simply meeting up at the court house to get it finished. He didn't think it was rushing things, but sometimes, he knew that Taylor did. He didn't have an opinion either way and was just glad that she was willing to meet him there to get their vows read and their marriage certificate filed. The sooner, the better he thought, what with her mother acting out.

He'd realized after talking to his older sister, Dakota, that Gilda was acting like a child more than an adult. It was as if what he'd been told all along. Gilda had had her every demand taken care of, and now that she was older, she expected the same thing to hold true. He didn't blame her parents for leaving her when they had. It must have been hard on them having a grown woman that needed her nose wiped and her food prepared for her.

Dakota also talked to him about using his place as a base for her catering business. Dakota Luncheon had been a huge hit back home, her bringing in sandwiches or whatever they wanted into corporate business meetings and then cleaning up when it was over. She'd also been doing a few graduations too that would want someone else to take over the food end of a party.

"I'll make sure that I'm not using your kitchen every day. I need to get my own building taken care of, but I wanted to see how well you were doing before I did that. You testing the water for me has given me a great deal of confidence that I didn't have before." He told her that he'd not gotten the nights opened up so far, but that was coming soon. "Good for you. I knew you were going to be a success. You just have a knack about you that tells people that you're going to give them really good food."

"Thanks. When do you think you'll start?" She told him she had a luncheon on Thursday afternoon with canapés and desserts. "Are you going to use the things we have here? I don't mind but if you do take something out, please make sure that you make a note of it. I don't want to be without something when I think that it's there."

"I will. I'm mostly just going to use things that I can get for a discount at the local stores. I understand that you've been looking into finding smaller items like to-go bags that will help you. I have stuff like that already. We can share resources on that if you want." He loved that idea and told her that. "Great. I'll be in tomorrow morning to get everything ready to go by the time you come in for your lunch crowd."

"We're closed on Thursdays. I'll come in to help you out if that's all right with you. That way,

I can get a good eye on what you will be doing and help you get it along so that it doesn't cost as much in labor." She told him that she was thinking of getting a nice truck to cart hot things in, too. "Great idea. I've been asked if we were going to do something like that at the county fairs and such. We can have some family fun together while we're at it."

After talking to his sister for a bit more, he was ready to go home. After getting the kitchen back to its usual neatness, he locked up and headed to his car. He was glad that he was looking around, something that he rarely did when he was headed home because he saw Gilda before she saw him.

Jack noticed that she was dressed in a sort of childish way. While she wasn't a bad-looking woman, she did have these things about her that made him wonder if she was sane. The short shorts she had on where something that he was sure that someone about half her age wouldn't be caught in, as well as the halter top that was a dizzying shade of orange and blue that made him slightly cross-eyed if she moved too quickly. Her hair was a tangled mess of a bun in the back, and her shoes, sandals, he supposed, were just flat pieces of foam that laced up her legs all the way to her thigh.

In that moment, he thought of his mother and how she had been dressed when she'd been called before Ronan as king. The same inappropriateness as his mother had been. He also thought that the two of them were alike in their wanting everyone to cater to their needs. Jack wanted to talk to his brothers and see what they thought.

He watched her as she roamed around the parking lot that his car was in. She stopped by it twice but didn't bother it. When she looked around, ducking behind a large truck, he made himself known to her in the event that she was going to key another car, thinking that it was his.

"What do you think you're doing?" She glared at him, and seeing her dressed as she was, it just made him laugh. "You don't frighten me any. Get yourself away from here so that you don't cause or get yourself into any more trouble."

"Where is Taylor? And Henrietta? Someone told me that she wasn't going to ever die. I demand that you give me whatever it was that they have. I deserve to live forever, too." He told her that he didn't know what she was talking about. "Sure you don't. I want you to find my daughter while you're at it. I know that she thinks that she's going to be marrying soon, but I have a few rules that I'd like to go over with the two of you before that."

"We're going to be getting married soon, as a matter of fact, and if you were going to ask, no, you're not invited. It's going to be a small ceremony of just a couple of people." Gilda told him she'd see about that. "You keep thinking that you're in charge. What did you want Taylor for? She's working in the event that you didn't know that."

"She's always been stupid about stuff like that. Working when there was plenty of money to go around. I haven't worked a day in my life. People just like to see me relaxed and happy." She glared at him after a few seconds, and it made him laugh. "Don't you want to see me happy...err... what is your name anyway? Not that I really care, but if I have to take you out of the picture, then I will. I've no idea why you think that you and Taylor have anything going on when she's been taking care of my needs since her father died. He was about useless, too."

"I'm Jack." He didn't tell her his last name on purpose. There is no telling what she'd do with that sort of information. He was slightly afraid of her. Gilda was unhinged, and there was no telling what she'd do if she got mad enough. "I can tell

Taylor or Henrietta that I spoke to you if you want. I'm not sure where she is right now, but I know she had plans for the rest of the afternoon."

"You tell them that it's high time we had a meeting. I don't like the way that I'm being treated, either. I should be first and foremost in their minds before anyone else. You tell them that I'm upset because things aren't being done for me." He nearly laughed but didn't. Gilda really was unhinged. "And I'm telling you this right now. There will be no children when you think to be married. I'm going to be at your house all the time to make sure that she never forgets her birth control. Taylor doesn't need children. She has me."

"You think that will work, do you? How do you propose to be at our home daily when we have no intentions of inviting you there? We're going to find us a nice place that you know nothing about and keep you out of our lives." She lunged at him, and he did take a step back, knowing that she couldn't reach him where he was standing but was hoping that she'd fall on her ass. When she fell against the car in front of her, he knew that she'd hurt herself. Instead of going to her aid, all he could think about was an injured bear and how it would attack. He got into his car and drove away. He didn't have any more time to waste on the other woman. She was going to be the police problem as soon as he could get someplace that he could call them.

"I believe that she keyed my future wife's car this morning and was looking for mine in the lot behind Jack's, too. I'll pay for any damage that she's done in the parking lot now but I'm not going to be so generous if she continues to be out and about causing trouble." Joey told him that he'd had to run her off this morning as she was hanging out at the Tucker Charity, looking for him. "I wondered how long it would take her before she would figure out that I'm a part of that as well. It did take a bit longer than I thought, to be honest."

"I've been keeping an eye on Ms. Murphy too. Now, that is a classy lady. She's been doing a lot for this town since I became a cop here. When she figured out that someone was tailing her, she told them it was all right to be with her but they weren't to get hurt if they could help it. I love that woman." He said that he did as well. "We know that Taylor is in her offices this morning and have been driving by there a few times a day. She always waves at us and doesn't fuss at us for wasting tax payer's money. I hear you're going to be getting married to her soon."

"Tomorrow morning at the court house. We just want to get it done so that there aren't any more problems with her mother. I hope that works anyway." He told him good luck with that. "Yeah, I understand that too."

Heading to the offices where both Henrietta and Taylor were working today, he was glad to see that they were having a snack to keep them tied over until dinner. He sat down to join them just as they were getting themselves something to drink.

~*~

Taylor watched her mother as she walked up and down in front of the Murphy Building. She didn't enter, for which she was happy but she did gesture towards the building and flip off anyone who came in or out of the building if she happened to be near enough. Grandma had told her that she thought that her mom was in a blind rage and that it would be better to let her stew rather than to try and figure out what she was pissed off about.

"Ms. Taylor? You have a call on line two. It's the man that you had a meeting with this morning, and he missed it." She asked if he had said why he missed it. "No. But he is upset that he doesn't have a check in his possession for the amount that he said you owe him."

"I'll take it. Also, Jack is supposed to come in today. Can you show him where my office is?" She smiled and said that she could. Picking up the phone, she realized something else. "The recording is still on about how whoever calls is being recorded, correct?"

"Yes, and I reminded Mr. Chou of it as well when he started cursing at me. A heads up, ma'am, he's spitting mad about something." Taking a deep breath, she smiled so that she'd at least start out on her end in a better mood. Whomever he was talking to was being fired and her heart hurt for the other woman. She might even try to find her and rehire her from the bully. When there was a lull in his berating the other woman, she spoke.

"Mr. Chou, it's Taylor Murphy Tucker. What is it I can do for you?" She waited a few seconds until he realized that she was on the line. "We had a meeting planned for this morning and you didn't show. That's not the way I do business."

"Where is my money?" She asked him what money he was talking about. "The money that you're going to pay me so that I don't buy you out lock stock and barrel."

"I wasn't aware that my business was up for sale. It didn't hit the paper where I'd think that sort of news would be. Perhaps you could explain it to me." He screamed that she owed him for not giving him the line of credit that he'd asked for. "I suppose you would think that with our last meeting but I remember telling you that there wasn't any way that I was going to give you any money to expand as you have no place to work on that as of now. You were to show me the land specs as well as the builders so that we can get started on that. As it is now, I'm not inclined to give you anything. I don't like to have my day messed up because someone didn't feel like coming to a meeting that we've set up."

"I've been doing business with your grannie for a long time. She never wanted to have meetings with her. She would come out to where I needed her and then set things up for me while she was here." Taylor reminded him, not for the first time, that she wasn't her grandmother. "No, you're not. She knew how to run a business. And you don't have the first clue on how to treat someone when they want to make you money."

"Mr. Chou, I believe my grandmother told you the last time she was with you that if you didn't pay the note on time, we would not be doing business with you. I've told you this as well. You borrowing twenty-three million off of us doesn't make us any money when you are already fifty-seven million dollars in arrears. That's not even counting the leans that we have against your company and the late charges that you owe. You're already in debt with us for over ninety million, and you've not made a payment in over six months."

"I was going to get caught up with you when you came here." She asked him if he was planning to use the expansion money to get caught up. "Yes. That's the way things work."

"So you'd use the expansion money that you told me you needed so badly because your lines were too slow to get partially caught up on the money that you already owe us?" He told her again that was how things worked. "I don't think so. If you don't expand like you said you needed to—and I agree with you—you're never going to get ahead of the losses that you're experiencing now. Me putting any of my money into your business would be like throwing gas on a fire. There will be nothing left for me when all is said and done. I'm afraid—and to be honest with you, I am afraid of your business failing. I'd be losing more money than you if I were to help you out like that."

"So you're not going to help me out?" She told him that she didn't think anyone would be willing to help him out with the track record that he has now. "Where is your grandmother? Now her I can talk to. She knows when things need to be put in place to handle the flow of business."

"My grandmother turned this over to me because she didn't want to deal with your lies anymore about your business. I've done some major research on you, Mr. Chou, and I've found out that you've been turned down by every bank in town. Not only that, but you've been playing the races and losing more than you can afford. Your wife has left you when you drained your retirement dry and left her with nothing of the money that her parents left her. Even she thinks this is a bad idea." He asked when she'd spoken to his wife. "Just this morning. She came to the meeting that you and I were to have this morning. She came here to convince me that doing business with you isn't going to help at all but to make both of us lose money. And I hate to lose money."

Her cell phone dinged, telling her that things were set up on the other end. Smiling, feeling good about the next steps that were going to befall Mr.

Chou, she leaned back in her chair just as Jack came into her office with her grandmother.

"As of this moment, Mr. Chou, the police are there to take your building away from you for nonpayment. The IRS is there because you've not paid your taxes in the last fifteen years as well as the land and property taxes on your personal property." He called her a cunt. "That's not all that nice, you know. Good luck in the future with your business, Mr. Chou. It looks like I'm going to be getting some, if not all, of my money back sooner than I thought."

"You've had him arrested then?" Taylor told her grandmother that his wife had brought in all the paperwork that she'd had at home about her husband and told her that he needed to have prison time. "That man could talk a big game, but he never had anything to back it up. That's why I gave it over to you. I knew you'd not waste any time with his ass. Stupid man. Who did he think that he was dealing with?"

"Stupid women. His wife, now, if she'd come in for a loan, I would have given it to her. Perhaps not, but I would have thought it over a great deal." Her cell phone rang, and she turned it off. "Speaking of stupid people. That was Mother.

She's been calling me about fourteen times a day now and leaving messages nastier than the last one."

"She is going on about us not having any children and that she's going to be at our home to make sure that you take your birth control every day. I didn't tell her that it wouldn't do any good. If you're in heat or ovulating, nothing can stop me from impregnating you." He explained how that would work. "I'm not saying that we start on children right away, but would you like a couple dozen?"

They all started laughing, and Taylor hugged him to her. She was so in love with this man that there were times when she thought someone should pinch her to make it all seem nothing like a dream. After going over the next day's schedule, they headed to her grandmother's home for dinner. She was going to have to talk to her grandmother about having Jack stay with them, him sleeping with her, but she'd not gotten around to it.

"I've been thinking. You should both move into this place on a permanent basis. It's not like there isn't enough room and I'd so love to have you both here all the time. When Jack leaves, it's like a part of my heart goes with him." Taylor looked at Jack and asked him if he'd like to stay there. "Oh, do say you will. I was also thinking that it might be a bit safer for the three of us if we were to stick together. There is no telling what that woman would do if she caught us unawares. My goodness, I just don't know what's come over her."

"She's realizing that her daughter is pulling away from her." When Parker popped into the room, he stood up. After introductions were made, he then explained that he'd gotten in touch with her about the magic that was in the family. "You were right in assuming that Jack healed your cancer. I'm here to offer you immortality as well. Jack and Taylor already have it, thanks to them being mates."

"Immortality? Is there such a—never mind you'd not say it if it wasn't true. I don't know what that means for someone as old as I am. Will I suddenly become younger? No, that's not right." Grandma looked at her and winked. "What would you say about having this old woman around all the time? I'll assure you that I'll not be in your bedroom in the morning to make sure that you're not popping the wrong sort of drugs."

"You're a hoot. It would be a pleasure to

have you around a bit more. But no, you won't be younger, but you will benefit from the magic that will come with it. You won't die, nor will you have the aches and pains of someone your age either." Parker took her grandmother's hands into hers. "You're completely cancer-free, and it won't be anything that comes around anymore, either. You can still get hurt, but you'll heal a great deal faster. No colds, either. You're going to be healthy as a person half your age."

"And what happens if I decide that I no longer want to be around? Is that something — I'm not saying that I'm going to do that, but will I be able to die should I want to? I've been around for a good long time, Parker, and I might just be sick of living with the world." Parker told her that she could take it away with just a snap of the fingers. "That will kill me?"

"No, you'll age a bit, not quickly, but your age, whatever it might be, will catch up to you. You'll more than likely die with your family surrounding you, and that would be nice, wouldn't it?" Nodding, Taylor felt her own eyes fill with tears about what was being said to her grandmother. "However I would like to suggest with the things that are going around right now with Gilda, you might well need the extra bit of magic, at least until she's gone."

"You know she's going to cause trouble then?" Parker said that she was too off her noodle not to be able to cause a great deal of trouble. "I worry about what I could have done when my grandson was around. He tried to tell me what she was like, and I didn't listen."

"It is his fault that things progressed more than they should have for him. And you were right in your thoughts that she drove him to his heart attack. Had she been a different person, or him a stronger man, they wouldn't have lasted the first few weeks of their marriage. But complete blame lies with her parents. She was a willful child, and they allowed her to have anything and everything that she wanted. Not many people will know this but they were afraid for Henry to marry their child. They knew what sort of person she was and didn't warn him about things that could have saved them both. Gilda should have been put in a home long before now. Or some kind of institution. She's not right." Parker looked at her. "You were but a child when she wanted you to take care of her. Since you knew no better than what she was when you were so young, you did what was necessary to make sure that you were well taken care of even if she didn't. It isn't your fault. I believe that had your father lived, he would have eventually left her and taken you with him. I doubt that your life would have been as good as it is right now, but I don't know for sure. As the old saying goes, you are what you were raised to be. You should be commended on how you turned out, Taylor."

After she left them, telling Jack and herself that the magic would only get stronger after they made love, Parker took her aside. After a quick hug, she looked her in the eye.

"Don't let her bully you into anything. Jack will never love anyone but you, so if you leave him because you're worried about him, remember this, if nothing else. You're immortal. Both of you are." She asked if she knew something more. "I do. Just bits and pieces, but don't let your mother bully you into anything."

"I won't." After she left them, her grandmother was talking to Jack. Interrupting just to make things clear, she smiled at her grandmother and Jack. "You're staying here. And we're going to have sex. A lot of it."

Grandmother cheered and then laughed. Jack stood and bowed before her before pulling her into his arms and kissing her. Life, their life, was about to get much more exciting. They'd deal with her mom when the time was right. But for now, they had each other.

Chapter 4

"I've never had sex before. I mean, I've been close but never wanted to go through with it. I think the few men that I dated thought that I was odd and didn't want to mess with me. That's what one of them said. They didn't want to mess with my virginity." He started to laugh, thinking that she had to be joking. Inhaling deeply of her, he knew what she said to be true. She'd saved herself for him. "So if I disappoint you, I'm so very sorry. I don't have any experience like you might well have."

"Never. You could never disappoint me in any way, shape, or form. You're all mine. Those other men need to be beaten. I want to kiss you, love." She nodded and wrapped her arms up and around his shoulders. Unlike most women he knew, she was tall and seemed to be the perfect fit against him. Breasts to chest and groin to groin. Flawlessly fit.

When she opened her lips Jack slowly

reached out and cupped both cheeks in his large hands and tilted her head at a better angle to the light. He studied her intently, moving her head this way and that to watch the light reflect off of her brilliant amber-colored eyes. He looked down at her then, really looked at her face when he saw her tongue slip out from between her lips and lick them moist. And if that was not enough to make him groan, she worried her full lower lip with her teeth. He watched the whole process with great fascination.

"Are you satisfied?" Her whispered, innocent question brought an immediate response from his already hardened cock. He could tell her in a word just how unsatisfied he was at the moment but could not make his throat work around the sudden dryness of his mouth. He wanted her with every fiber of his being. And he was suddenly very glad he was holding her. He was sure that if he wasn't, she would leave him.

"Why?" Her voice was husky and smooth as she spoke like she'd read his mind. "Why would you think that I'd leave you now? You're all I know, all I want in this world. I never knew that love could be so consuming, so lasting. I love you, Jack. I love all of you."

She licked her lips again. Her own body was responding to his closeness, and he could smell her arousal. He watched her eyes become a darker shade of amber, more brilliant in their color as the moments passed, and he touched her.

"I need to know your full name so that I can taste it on my lips. Have it fill my soul. Tell me, please. Tell me your name so that I can cherish you forever."

"It's...it's Taylor. Taylor Ann Murphy. I want you to step back away from me. You...you're making me nervous. You have to...you need to... please Jack, I..." She took a step back and then another. She could still touch him, but it wasn't as overwhelming as it had been. She could breathe again.

"I'm sorry, love. I truly am. I want you so very much. I'll calm myself down a bit." His mouth brushed hers once more, and then he touched his mouth to hers and deepened it to a kiss. His slow possession of her made her feel better. Less overwhelmed as she had been before. As he kissed her, it was more than before. Like he was marking her with his mouth.

His kiss demanded a response from her, and he got it. There was no timid response from her this time or between them. With his hand still on her cheeks, he pressed her mouth open for his and tasted her. He captured her groan as it rumbled from deep and moved across his tongue like a taste, a taste like ambrosia. Jack shifted her body to his left and used his right hand to cup her ass against him, tightening her hard against him. Lifting her feet up off of the floor, Jack felt her pour over him.

Never had he felt this way about sex or a woman. No, he realized, not sex. This had moved beyond just sex. This was a claiming, he needed to claim her. Shifting her again, he ran his hands along her thighs and helped her wrap those incredible legs around him. He was not going to take her here for as much as he wanted to. He needed to make love to her in his lair, in his bed.

Jack, with Taylor wrapped around him, moved to the panel in the far wall that would take them to the higher levels and opened it. The trip took them longer because neither could stop touching, kissing exposed flesh, and marveling at new tastes. He'd had to try several times to get his door to open because he kept losing his concentration on an otherwise easy task.

Finally, the door sprang open, and he pulled her close again and moved into the room. With a swift kick, the door slammed and locked behind them. He wanted to slow down. He wanted to rip her clothes off and take her while standing there. He wanted to taste her slowly, savor her body. He also wanted to sink his cock deep inside of her, fuck her until neither of them could stand. His body ached. His need was incredible.

"Taylor, I need you baby. Tell me. Tell me that you need me as well. I want to hear you say it. Tell me."

He cupped her breast through the shirt she had on and knew that she was bare beneath it. His already heated blood felt as though lava was racing along his veins through him. He felt her arch into his palm, the nipple hard against his thumb. He bent down and took it into his mouth, nipping at her nipple through the material, soaking it through.

When her approval of a hissed yes spilled from her mouth, Jack felt as though he could take on the world. She pulled him closer to her breast by grabbing a handful of his hair and holding him there. Her hips began to move against his groin and his cock, making it difficult for him to think.

Jack could smell her more now. Her arousal was hot and heavy, making him crazy with need. He reached between them and yanked his shirt in half, buttons from the front flying all over the room. Hers was next. The thin material of her tee shirt didn't stand a chance against this primal need to be with her. This time, when he suckled at her breast, he tasted her skin, the heady taste that was unique to her.

He moved up her neck and along her jaw, nipping still and sucking on her hot flesh. Her body was as on fire as his. He pulled her lower body from his and heard her whimper. He knew how she felt, but it would be worth the moment of separation as he pulled the snap open to her pants and slid the zipper down. She soon got the idea and began working the belt loose to get to his button as well. By the time he had managed to get his hands down the back of her pants and cupped her bare ass again, she had his pants undone and was now stroking his cock through his briefs. The bed, even at three feet away, was too far. They would never make it, he thought with a grin. And if she kept touching him as she was now, he was not going to last much longer anyway.

Dropping to his knees before her, he stripped her of the rest of her clothing. Standing before him was the most magnificent sight he had ever had the pleasure of gazing upon.

He looked up at her and saw that her eyes had turned and were now glowing from something within. His own eyes had turned as well. He could see her through the darkened haze of his heightened state of need. Running his hands up her legs to her thighs, he never stopped looking at her face as she spoke to him.

"I'm going to taste you, love you with my mouth until you scream my name over and over." He flicked his finger up the seam of her nether lips. "Here, here is where I'm going to taste you." He could feel her heat. See the wetness gathering in the curls there. Slowly, he inserted his finger into her, stretching her, widening and separating his fingers as he pumped them in and out of her, into her heat and wetness. When she started to close her eyes, he stopped her.

"Taylor, honey, watch me, watch me as I stretch you for me. I'm going to bury my cock deep inside of you, feel you wrap around me. I'm going to ready your body for me. Then I'm going to fuck you, make you mine. Watch me."

When she focused again, he slowly inserted another finger deep into her again. He watched her, her body undulating up and down against his hand and fingers, her juices coating him.

"That's it, baby. Feel me inside you. Christ, you're so hot. And you're wet, so wet for me. I need to taste your cream."

Jack pulled out his finger and stuck it into his mouth, moaning loudly at the honeyed taste of her. When he had licked and sucked his finger dry of her, he leaned forward and kissed her thighs, first one, then the other. Her need was evident in her scent, her needy response to him and her body, making him dizzy with an overwhelming need to claim.

He inserted his fingers again and leaned in to lick at her. His tongue joined his fingers, and he fucked her with his mouth, never touching her clit until he was sure she was ready for him. He removed his fingers from her and pulled her thighs further apart, giving him more room to taste her. Just as he sucked her clit into his mouth and teased it with his tongue, he pumped harder into her, stroked her hard, then softly over and over, flatting his tongue against her clit. He couldn't seem to get enough of her and wondered if he ever would.

She was so close. Her cries and moans filled his head. He could feel her reaching her peak. He wanted to taste it, her first time. He needed to taste her come for him.

"Come for me, baby, let go and come now." Her legs tightened down hard around his head, and she rode his mouth. When she came, she screamed, her body pulsing around his finger and mouth.

He lapped at her tender flesh, bringing her to peak twice more as he did. He wanted her now. His cock was aching to be inside of her. He gently guided her to the floor. Jack leaned over her lax body and looked at her.

"I want you, baby. I want to be inside of you so badly I ache. I need to be inside of you."

Jack moved up and between her legs. He kissed her tenderly and completely. He needed to slow down. He realized his size and her virginity would be a painful combination for her first time. And he did not want her first time to be marred by a painful memory.

"Please, Jack, I need you. I want you inside of me, please." Her begging nearly tore him apart, but he knew she would love him more if he remained strong.

"I know, love, but I don't want to hurt you. We need to go slowly this time." He moved up and positioned his cock at the core of her and moved slowly into her. He felt her stiffen beneath him, and he stopped. "All right? Am I hurting you?" He knew at that moment if she asked him to stop, he would. At this moment, if she asked him to do anything, he would die giving it to her.

"No, you feel so good there. I want more. Please give me more of you, all of you." She moved up to meet his downward push. He stopped when he met with her maidenhead. He looked down into her eyes and fell in love.

"You...this will hurt, baby, I'm so sorry." And he slammed forward, quick and hard, into her. She jerked back against the bed when he broke through, and she tried to get away from him.

"Shhhh, baby, it's all right. I'm so sorry, Taylor. I promise you that I didn't mean to hurt you. I will never hurt you again. Shhhh. I have you."

He did not move his body, afraid of hurting her more. He just held her tightly to him and cooed softly into her ear. He petted her, touched her tenderly, and gave her comfort. When he felt her relax again, he moved slowly back and into her again.

"Jack, please."

He reached down and grasped her hip,

then slipped his hand beneath her, cupping her ass and tilting her upward, allowing him to slide deeper into her. He felt her legs rise and encircle his thighs, pushing up against him with each downward stroke. He was close to coming. He could feel his balls rise and tighten against him. His lion stretched beneath his skin, his need to taste her, to mark her imminent.

"Taylor, I want to taste you. I need to taste you now." He moved his mouth along her jaw, nipping. He found her pulse and suckled it into his mouth. He could feel the blood pounding through her jugular.

"Yes, Jack, please take me. Take all of me."

He kissed her where he would bite her, licked the pulse again to take away most of the pain, and bit down. Her blood filled his mouth. Her power and the power of her essence roared through him. He drew hard on her vein and came.

His climax reverberated through him, gripping him hard. He poured into her, deep and completely, touching her womb with each hard thrust. She rolled over the edge of completion with him, her body like a silken sheath. It held him. He felt her milking and pulling him deeper into her. When he was spent, he collapsed on top of her, barely able to roll to the side at the last second and pull her atop him as he went. He did not as much as fall asleep but drifted into unconsciousness along with her.

~*~

Taylor watched the evening sun as it fell behind the trees in their yard. Her entire body had been tingling all day, since before she got up, leaving Jack in bed. Her shower was quick and quiet. Body aching so that when she opened the medicine cabinet, she nearly sobbed in relief when she found some over-the-counter medication for sore muscles. Hers were about as sore as she'd ever felt this morning. But she did feel really good about everything else.

Now, she was sitting on the deck in the unseasonable warm weather with just a pair of shorts on and a sloppy tee shirt. Thinking about Jack seemed to be all her mind could center on today. Almost as if she summoned him, he kissed her on the mouth and sat on the lounger with her. He had taken advantage of the warmer weather with a pair of shorts and a tee shirt that had seen better days about ten years ago. He asked her how she was doing.

"I have this little bit of humming going on,

but other than that, I feel really good. I've been enjoying the day too. How are you feeling today?" He took her hand into his and kissed the back of it.

"How do I feel?" He did look like he was feeling well but the moment that he moved her leg for more room, all thoughts of that went out the door. "I'm right there with you. It's like my body is humming about something, too. I thought that it was tingling, but you're right. It's humming. I've never felt this way before."

"You mean after sex or just in general." He told her after mind-blowing sex. "I don't have a great deal to compare that to, but I'd say you got that right. I didn't wake you, did I? I know a few times when I was washing up, I moaned a bit more than I could catch."

"You didn't wake me. I think I was dead to the world. I slept good, too. I don't know that I ever moved once after you making love with me." Her face heated up, she could feel the heat of it on her hands when she went to cool them. "You're extremely beautiful. And delicious, too. Like fine chocolate and a great wine. As much as I'd like to take you again, I think that we should wait a bit. How about that?"

"I like being compared to wine and chocolate.

It's better than an old maid and a spinster. But yes, a few days of rest will be just great. Did I tell you that I've been called that a couple of times?" He asked who had said it to her. "What happens if I tell you their name? What will you do?"

"Hunt them down and kill them." She wasn't sure if he was joking or not. There was something very scary about the look on his face. Just as she was ready to ask him if he was kidding or not, he spoke again. "I have to go to work in about an hour. I need to put in an order for the restaurant and do the books. Nearly everyone pays by credit card now, but I pay my staff their tips the next morning. So far they don't seem to complain too much about that, the staff I mean. Next week, on Monday, it'll be the first dinner we serve besides that to my family."

"Can I make a suggestion?" He told her that he would love for her to. "I love the little basket of teas that you hand out. I don't drink it, so maybe this is dumb, but just having one flavor might not be a good thing. My grandma doesn't drink black tea after a certain hour because of the caffeine. Put other flavors and decaf in the little basket, too."

"Good idea. I love that. My grannie won't drink tea after six. She said she's up and down too much. Something else that was suggested was creamer with the tea and coffee, not the non-dairy stuff that most places have.

"That sounds a little classy, don't you think?" He explained to her that he wasn't going for classy but for comfort food. He said that creamer to him would be a comfort over the little cups of dried creamer would be. "I suppose so. I think that if I were going to drink any of them, I'd want the real creamer as well."

After he left her, she continued to sit out on the deck. She was surprised when her grandma found her to learn that she'd been back there for nearly four hours. It had been nice and quiet with just the trees and plants for company. Now, her grandma was like a cherry on the top of a banana split.

"I've heard from Hudson, and my changes have been made. Now all I have to do is go and sign it so that it can be filed." Taylor asked her if she was happy with the changes. "I am. Knowing that I'm not going to overly burden you with all the extra work does make me feel better. And speaking of which, I've decided to go on a cruise for a month. I've not done anything like that in decades and I think that I'd enjoy getting away while Gilda is getting taken care of. Did you hear that she's demanding a larger condo? I thought that she had about the biggest one they had in that development."

"She wants me to have one built for her that has several bedrooms so that she has room to spread out. I don't know what she'd be spreading out for; she rarely leaves the living room, and I don't believe that she's ever been in the kitchen of any place that she's lived in." Grandma asked her what she wanted to do. "To be honest, I have no idea. I'm angry with her so much that I want to cut all ties with her. She needs to grow up." She didn't say anything.

Leaning her head on the back of the lounger, she was happy that, for now, at least the subject was finished. She knew that she was going to have to deal with her sooner or later, but for now, she was going to rest and regroup. Something that she'd not done in a very long time.

When she woke up, she realized that at some point, Jack or someone had brought her into the house and laid her on the couch. Jack was lying on the other couch in the huge living room, apparently reading a book. She sat up and had to lie back down quickly. She was about as light-headed as she'd been in a very long time.

"Are you all right?" She said that she didn't know. "While you were sleeping, I made some discoveries about my own magic. You have some as well. I didn't bring you in here but you just disappeared from the porch to the couch. I think you got chilled or something. Anyway, I'd gotten back about an hour ago, and that's when I was going to bring you in."

"Did you do that, or did I?" He said that he was pretty sure that it was her. "I see. I don't really, but I'm trying my best to figure out why I'm so dizzy."

"It's the magic for when we came together as a couple." Sitting up, she looked at him. "Are you better now?"

"I think so. It's a great deal to take in, don't you think?" He got up off the couch he was on and sat with her on the one that she was on. "I'm feeling better, but I have this strange feeling of being two different people. Like, I have a cat right there with me. Is that possible?"

"I don't see why not." That wasn't all that helpful, and she told him that. His laughter made her smile. He really was such a wonderful person, and she loved him so much. "There is very little that we know of in taking mates. My grandparents raised us when my parents abandoned us one year. They were old then, I remember thinking, but they didn't have much to say about how our parents just dropped us off one day and took off."

"Well, that just sucks." He laughed again. "Where are they now? I'm assuming that they're living the grand life without all of you guys around. By the way, that was sarcasm. I hope that they're not having a good time at anything."

"They're both dead." She felt her face heat up, and she couldn't tell him quickly enough how sorry she was. "Don't be. They got what they deserved, and I'm happy for it. I didn't know them all that well. I was only about six or so when they did that. But they'd been called before Ronan, the king of our kind, and he had them destroyed by the leap—that's what you call a bunch of lions. Also a pride. Anyway, they're both gone and I find that I'm not the least bit sorry about it. They actually blamed us for being born. That pissed us off so much that we had to regroup and think about that. Ten children are a lot, but they could have stopped at any time."

"My mom sounds like she could have been related to them. She's always been selfish and childish. I know that it's not my fault but that of her own parents, but I was stuck with her when my dad died. I don't know what I would have done if Grandma hadn't taken us in. Still raising her, I guess." He asked her if she was going to be upset if her mother spent some time in jail. "No. I mean, they'll treat her like all the other prisons and that will be good for her. I'm not saying that she'll like it, but I really don't care anymore. I'm worried that she'll try and hurt you or one of your family members, but I have to keep telling myself that we're all immortal and we can't die."

"You can be hurt, however. So I want you to be extra careful when she's around. Maybe when she's not around. I've noticed that she can be pretty sneaky when she's looking for someone to help her." She nodded because that was what Parker had explained to her and her grandmother. "I know you have to go to the groundbreaking. Just make sure that you're never alone. I'll be there too, but I will be a little late. I have to have someone wait for the truck to come in with our food stuffs on it. It'll be early, but you never know what's going to happen when a truck comes in."

She'd nearly forgotten about that. The distribution center was going to be bringing in all her products for the little mom and pop stores she had all over the state and have it separated out for each store. It was going to save time at the stores because they no longer had to have several trucks a week come in for goods but one truck that would bring in everything at once. Sodas were the only thing that would be coming in separately, and that would be set up by the vendor. It was going to be better than she thought.

There would be kinks to work out, and she was aware of that. But to have everything arriving at once would cut down on labor costs as well as getting larger quantities delivered sooner without the cost of several trips by the vendor. She was looking forward to that as much as she was seeing the first store receive their goods. And she'd be there, too. Just like she was going to be at the groundbreaking in the morning. She couldn't believe that it was finally happening.

The specialized car warehouse was going to break ground in a couple of months. There were still a few things that had to be ironed out in the contract, but it would, along with her place, bring in over two thousand new jobs. The other warehouse was going to be building together break harness assembly and sending them to the bigger places to put into cars. It was going to be a win-win for everyone around town because they were offering new car discounts. She thought that was about the best incentive going.

Getting ready for dinner, she was happy to hear her grandma talking to Jack about the house and how it ran. It wasn't like he was going to take over someday, but he was curious, and Grandma loved to talk about how her dad had started the house on the way to where it was today. Her favorite part about the lawns was that he'd had the goats, twice a year, come into the front lawns and mow it down for nothing. That, too, was the main reason that none of them had ever been near any poison ivy, as the goats would strip down to the root and kill it. Even along the gates and gates around the compound were taken care of by the goats to this day. It was good for the air with no gas and also for the lawns as there were no chemicals sprayed around to get rid of it along the paths as well. Smiling when Grandma got to the part about the apples and how they were watered in the spring, she knew that Jack would be out there when the time came to make sure that it was going according to Grandda's plan.

Chapter 5

"I don't understand what this is." Taylor handed the certified mail to Jack and sat down when he read it over. "It looks like my mom is suing me for something. I can't think where she thinks I've stolen her money."

"She's saying that you never gave her half of the insurance money from when your father died. Also, she's claiming that she's never received any kind of compensation from his work. She's blaming it all on you and your grandmother." Taylor asked if she had realized that she'd only been three weeks old when her dad had died. "She doesn't say anything like that, no, but I think she's saying that you and your grandmother have had her on some kind of budget since you were old enough, and now she wants all her money."

"We tried that once before. About ten years ago. She wanted to have unlimited access to all the money that had been keeping her in money, and within a few days, she was nearly broke. I would love to give it all to her and say have at it." He told her that she should do that. "I'm sick of being my mother's keeper, Jack. It's like my whole life, I've been caring for her needs instead of my own. Now that I have you in my life, I just want to be the person that I should have been when I was a child. She never let me become the child but her constant caretaker all my life."

"What will your grandmother say? I'm sure that she got the same letter as you did." They found out that not only had Grandma gotten the letter, but she was just as pissed off about it as Taylor was. "It says here that the meeting will be in two days. Not a lot of time to get anything set up for it." She asked if Ivy could be her attorney. "You'd have to ask her. I can't see her having any trouble with it. She's having a good time being an attorney."

"I'll call her today. I have all the notes on how all the money was distributed. I also have the information on how the checks that came in were cashed and sent out as well. Mom and I were the benefactors on his insurance, leaving fifty grand to us both. It wasn't a great deal, not by today's standards, but with Grandma's help, I was able to make it into a couple of million before I turned eighteen." Jack told her that was great. "Mom hated it. Spending money to make more? She thought that she should have been allowed to have it all at once, then she'd be able to make her own investments. She changed her mind or something. I don't remember why she didn't get it all, now that I think about it."

"You said you tried once before to give her the money. How did that turn out?" Taylor told him what she remembered. "So she had all this money and didn't know what to do with it other than to buy expensive things? How did you get her on track again?"

"She begged us to keep her on a budget then. It was as if having the money overwhelmed her somewhat, and she couldn't take it." Taylor laughed. "She even had us take all the things that she'd purchased, mink coats, jewelry, and other high-end items that were still in their original bags back to get them out of her house. I don't know why she thinks this time will be any different."

"I'd make sure that I told Ivy that, too. I don't know that it matters other than she'd be in charge of her own things, but perhaps you could tell her that this is the last time you're going to bail her out." She told him that she'd already told her that the last time. "Good, then she can do what she wants. It will be one less thing that you have to worry about with her. I saw her in town the other day, and I was amazed at how bad she looked. It's like she's given up all sense of good manners and dressing. She had on a sweatshirt with something on the front of it, plus a pair of short shorts that were much too small for her frame. Almost like she'd given up on being well dressed."

"She's claiming that we've stolen everything from her, and she doesn't have the funds to do anything. Which is a lie. She has open accounts in every store along the main roads and a few specialized places like where she gets her hair and nails done. I don't know what's wrong with her." Jack pointed out a couple of things. "Yes, well, there is her trying to keep us apart. It hurts me a bit that she is so set on us not having children. I thought everyone wanted a couple of grandkids to have on their laps."

"You talk to Ivy, and I'll go downtown to Jack's Place. I'll have to go back there tonight for our dinner hours, but I don't anticipate being late. I want to go in now and make sure that things are set up correctly. I don't know that we'll be all that busy on our first night." She just smiled at him.

She thought that they'd be busy all night and would have a great deal of fun while they were at it. "Reach out to me if you need me. I'll have someone cover for me on Thursday for your court hearing. That way, I can go with you."

Instead of calling Ivy, she called her grandmother. She had been notified too about her mom wanting money, and it didn't bother her all that much either. Mom would be overwhelmed again and call them like she had the first time. Things were no different for her, except that she might well get overwhelmed quicker with her and Jack getting married and such. She couldn't understand why her mother was trying so hard to make everyone mad at her.

The two of them went over the paperwork that had made her able to trade on the open market. There was also a signed paperwork that said that her mother would allow her to make money for her on the same market. It was worded well, the attorney told them at the time, making it so that her mom nor any of them, for that matter ran out of money. She'd always been really good at investing and trading, but her mom had never seemed to care so long as when she wanted something, there was a way for her to get it. Ivy joined them just as they were finishing their lunch.

"I'd be glad to join you in this. I've been looking over all the paperwork that your grandmother sent me, and it doesn't seem to me that you've done anything untoward to her in what she considers theft of her money. Do you suppose that she simply wants to be involved more?" Grandma said she thought that Gilda thought that by wanting her money, she'd make them broke. "There isn't any way that she could make either of you broke. Henrietta, you had millions before Gilda was even born. Taylor, you own so many businesses and assets that there isn't any way that if she took what she thought should have come to her that it would make a dent into your money. What else could it be?"

"She doesn't want me to marry. Or for that matter to have anything to do with anyone that isn't her. Mom is dependent on me—selfishly I might add and won't allow me to have a life in the event that she needs something from me in the future. All my time and energy should be just for her, and she won't tolerate me having a life outside of her." Ivy said that was just silly. "But the truth. I've been taking care of her all my life. Even when I needed her to take care of me, her needs came first. Grandma and I have both been talking about it, and it has to do with the fact that her parents pampered her every need and now she's gotten used to it, there isn't any other way that it should be going. She demands that she live with Jack and me so that she can make sure that I don't have children that will distract me from her needs. She actually said that to us."

For the rest of the afternoon and into the evening, they talked about the case that her mother was bringing against them. At about six, Jack reached out to the family, saying that he was buried at work and needed all their help. Apparently his thoughts of not being all that busy didn't happen like he'd thought.

Everyone was going to go to Jack's to help out. Almost as soon as they pulled onto the street, they could see the lines of people waiting to get in. She and her grandma got out of the limo and ran to the back door of the place. Jack was standing at the back door like he was ready to bolt.

"There are over seventy people in the dining right now who are waiting on dinner. Then, there are as many as two hundred waiting to get inside to eat. Almost three hundred people are here to eat and standing in the chilly night to get some food. I don't know how I'm— Henrietta, did you just hit me?" She said that she had and would again if he didn't stop babbling. "I can't do this. I don't know that I even have enough food for all of them."

"Of course you can. Damn it, boy, get in there and start cooking. Just cook one ticket at a time until you get them all cleared off. Didn't that witchy woman make your walk-in special? Well, that doesn't sound to me like you're going to be running out of food anytime soon. Get in the kitchen before I have to start cooking. And I don't know a lick about cooking." He left the two of them standing there. "Do you think he's going to remember that I taught you how to cook, love?"

"Not tonight, he might not." They went into the kitchen to hear Jack telling his crew what to do. Basically, just wait on one table at a time until they were finished. Assigning his brothers as bus boys and two of them making salads to take out, it looked less like they were going to be in trouble and more like the family was going to be in over their heads. She and her grandma started chopping up the vegetables that were going to be needed for the grill, and they were set to go. When the first order came back, it was like a Zen or something laid over the kitchen. Not a sound was made that was loud, no one panicked when the salad bowl was temporarily empty, and when Denver took over as host, tables were being reseated in record time, and there was very little in the way of complaints made when people had to wait for an extra few minutes to have a seat to eat in the newest place in town.

It was well after midnight when the place was beginning to slow down. Thanks to the extra hands and the magic, they were able to feed all the people that had ventured out tonight. She noticed that everyone looked beat, but Jack decided to feed them all for helping out, including his staff and helped with the dishwashing that seemed to be never-ending. To her, it had been a good time. She didn't know how Jack was going to feel when he realized that he'd fed well over three hundred patrons, and not a one of them had been upset with the long waits if you weren't first in line.

"I think that I should have taken tonight more seriously." She laughed with Jack as he sat at the table in the kitchen with them. "I kept thinking that you guys were just ordering food to make me feel better. I snuck out once to look and the dining room was as full as I'd ever thought that it would be. There seemed to be no end to the amount of food that I was cooking."

"You're going to have to expand soon. Word has gotten out now that you're open, and I think that you're going to be busy like this all the time. I, for one, was hard-pressed not to take someone's plate of scallops and rice. There were so many compliments about it that I was sure you were going to run out, magic or not." Denver laughed. "People were so wonderful, Jack. They were willing to share tables with strangers rather than wait for a second table to open up. And six tops were full of people who were strangers to each other. You did good, little brother."

"I couldn't have done this without you guys. When I got here at noon, Shelby said that the reservations were full. I thought that she was joking. Then, when I went out to check on the tables at one point before I started cooking, I couldn't believe the place was standing room only for the tables that we had." Denver told him that he thought tomorrow night was full as well. "I'm going to need to hire more people. Not just to be inside, but the patio was a huge hit tonight, even though it wasn't all that warm out. I have to admit, I'm about as excited about a project as I've ever been. I can't wait to tell Grandma and Grandda.

They're going to get a kick out of this.

Taylor helped with cleaning the tables. After setting all the chairs on the tables, one of the waitstaff got out the vacuum and started cleaning up the floor. Grandma and Bailee took the flowers that had faired well back to the cooler for tomorrow and they all laughed about how they were all starving when they'd arrived and had eaten their fair share of bread while working.

Jack had picked a good staff. None of them had quit like she might have well done if she'd been sixteen and hit with this much business. But they all pulled together, had a great night with tips, and were eagerly excited about tomorrow night's business.

In two days, she was going to have to be in a courtroom with her mom and she found that she didn't care how it turned out. If her mom took what she thought that she had coming to her, it really would be one less thing that she had to worry about. Her mom was becoming a drain on her, and she wasn't sure if she could handle any more of her stress like she had over the last few weeks. Her mom was going to have to grow up, and she couldn't think of a better way for her to do so than to be in charge of her own money and life.

~*~

Selling her condo was going to be the first thing that she did. Gilda Jane had wanted a bigger place for some time now, and there was no reason for her to wait until the court said that she was rich. She was too. Simply because Taylor was. Her daughter would take care of her, and she'd have all her money, too. That was what she wanted and Gilda Jane wasn't going to let her marry either.

She didn't know why she wanted to marry someone anyway. She'd never cared for it, but her parents had made her get out of the house and do so, or they'd cut her off and kick her out. Marrying Henry Paul hadn't been a real hardship on her but he would tell her no more than she cared for. Then there was the baby.

She could have gone her entire life without getting pregnant. It made her body out of shape. Her feet and hands were always swollen. The doctor tried to make her do some exercises, but she didn't want the baby, much less getting her body ready to deliver it. And good Christ, having the kid nearly killed her. There was never going to be any way that she was going to do that again. It was too painful and messy. But Henry Paul thought that the baby was adorable. She wasn't.

Her face was forever pinched-looking. Her hands and feet were so small that she thought that there was no way that it would ever be able to use them. Also, Taylor had been born with a full head of blond hair that never fell out like she'd been told it would. Taylor had more hair appointments than she did right after birth.

Then, her husband had died. All his promises about him caring for the thing went out the door when she woke one morning with him lying beside her dead. It wasn't fair. She'd not wanted it in the first place now she had her all the time, day and night. No, she thought, it wasn't fair that people, especially Henrietta, would fawn all over the child while she was sitting right there. No one, after Taylor was born, wanted to do a damned thing for her, not even to take her shopping so that she could get herself some new things.

She remembered one time when her mother had set her up with a babysitting job. It had been the little girl down the street, and she was, she supposed, about four years old. Gilda Jane had only stayed at the house for twenty minutes before she decided that the kid was too needy and left her there all alone. The little girl called the police, and she'd gotten into a bit of trouble with that, but her mom never set her up with a babysitting job again. She couldn't stand kids.

"You're not a good child, are you, Gilda Jane?" She told the officer that it wasn't her fault that the kid needed things when Gilda hadn't wanted to get them for her. "You were supposed to keep an eye on her. Leaving her alone could have gotten the child hurt or worse."

"Well then, I guess no one would have to babysit her again. I didn't want to go over there in the first place. My mom wouldn't come with me so that I could do what I wanted, so the kid got what she deserved." The officer looked shocked, and she shrugged. "When I go places people have to remember that I'm the one that should be taken care of. My needs come before anyone else's. That's the way it's always been, and it will always be like that. I don't like people getting more of anything more than I am."

"That's just selfish, Gilda Jane. What would you have done if she needed her dinner or even hurt herself? What would you have done for her?" She told him nothing. She'd just have to learn that Gilda Jane was far better than anyone and got what she wanted. Forever. And by golly, her daughter was going to have to learn the same thing. She came first in all things, and that included her time. She didn't want to have to be put second in her life that's why marrying that man was such a terrible idea. He'd want all her time and where would that leave her? Second. She didn't want to be second. It was Taylor's duty to make sure that she was first in everything that she did. Or she'd make her regret it.

The morning of the trial was set for two hours from the time she woke up. The first thing she was going to figure out was why she couldn't sell her condo. Since all her money was tied up in things that her daughter had figured out for her, the bank wouldn't allow her to purchase something else that was larger. Her daughter should have wanted her to have the best. Now, here she was, living in the same place without Taylor around to make sure that things were set up the way that she wanted. That didn't sit right with her, and she was going to make sure that the judge made it right, too.

The courtroom had too many people in it. She told the man standing at the door to get everyone out so that she could have the room all to herself. He told her that these people were here to support her daughter and that he wasn't going to make anyone leave. She'd just see about that.

It seemed to her that no one wanted her to have what she wanted, and heads were going to have to roll if things didn't straighten up.

"Mother." She looked at the woman at the table and didn't recognize her. There was something about her that made her think it was Taylor, but this woman was just too beautiful her skin seemed to glow. The smile on her face was nothing that she'd ever seen before. It was bright and beautiful. It wasn't until she spoke again that she realized that it was indeed her Taylor. "Why are you doing this? It's not going to get you anywhere."

"We'll see. You will either have to start taking care of me the way that I want, or I'm going to take all your money from you. And I have a list of things that you're going to do the first day that are just going to be the tip of the things that you're going to do for me. Just say that you'll do as I want, and I'll call this off. Otherwise you're going to see yourself in a very deep hole and still having to take care of me." She told her that she wasn't going to do that. "Because of that man you think you're going to marry? Is that what that is all about? I won't allow it, Taylor. You need to make sure that I have everything that I want. It's the way things should be going."

"No. However, if you go through with this, I'm going to drop everything that I do for you that you have no idea about. Like the condo and—" She said she was going to sell it and get something bigger. Just so the two of them could live together all the time. "You can't sell the condo because it doesn't belong to you. I own the entire subdivision. All the condos belong to me, and the only way that you can sell them is if I say so, which I won't. They're rentals, not ownership. It makes me more money that way, and I don't have to worry about them sitting empty when someone moves out."

"No, that's no right. I own it. I bought and paid for it." She didn't say anything, and she looked over at her attorney. She asked him if she owned it or not. "Well? Do I or do I have to get my daughter to turn it over to me?"

"I tried to tell you that you don't own anything. You have nothing to liquidate as it stands right now. You used to own a house that you didn't pay taxes on, so it was taken by the bank." Taylor said that she bought it when it went up for auction. "I figured as much. Also, there were two businesses that you owned that, too, were repossessed by the bank when you didn't pay any taxes on them."

"Taylor should have done that." He handed her a contract, but she wouldn't look at it. "What does it say? Just tell me."

"It says that if you didn't meet the demands of the business, which would include the taxes, then it would revert back to the original owner. That would be your grandmother-in-law, Harrietta Murphy. It was then sold to Taylor when things from the estate were put together into a single business. One that you signed off on that you wanted nothing to do with." She asked if she had any money from that. "As I have told you several times over the past few days, Ms. Murphy, you don't own anything. No stocks, no bonds, and certainly no capital from any of the businesses that you were supposed to have taken care of when you had them."

"Someone should have taken care of them for me. I didn't want to have to mess with things unless I wanted to. Why didn't someone tell me what to do?" Taylor told her mom that she had daily, that things needed to be taken care of. "Then you should have taken care of them for me. You know I don't like to be bothered with things like that. Unless all the attention is on me, I don't want anything to do with it."

"Well, it sucks to be you then." She told her to have respect for her, or she could make her life a living hell. "You've done that since I was a child. I didn't realize it, of course, because you've always been like this but I've been the parent in this since I was too young to understand that you were a selfish person."

"So? It's all right to be selfish. And that's not a word that I'd use for myself. I just want things to go my way, and there is no harm in that." Taylor told her that there were issues with that. No one had time to take care of her the way that she wanted. "My parents did it all right. And even your father until he got himself dead. He promised me riches and all he left me with was a baby that I couldn't stand. Not until you were older, anyway. All you did was want-want-want. Well, I had wants and needs, too, that should have been taken care of instead of you. You were nothing to me. I've wanted to say that to you for such a long time. If not for the fact that you got older and were able to do what I wanted, I would have just as soon that you died. I needed things to be going my way, and all people thought about was how you were such a pretty good baby. Nothing about me. I should have gotten all the attention and people doing what I wanted, not some brat who was as useless as my husband was when he promised to take care of you all the time if I just gave him children. Never again will I be duped that way."

"That's enough." Her mom told Jack to shut up. "I will not. My god, woman, do you really believe what you're saying? That you didn't like your daughter, much less your husband?"

"I just wanted to stay at home with my parents. They knew just how to treat me." He asked if she knew where they were. "No. They left me with Henry Paul the moment that we were married. And he didn't cater to me like they told me he would, either. He was so focused on making a living when he had all the money that we needed that he would leave me for hours on end to go to his work and leave me home. I didn't want to be left alone. There was no one around to make sure that I had all that I wanted. It's all about me, don't you understand? It must be just about me."

Taylor looked around the room. The judge had entered at some point, and he just stared at her mom, much like everyone else in the room was. She'd not only just admitted that she was selfish but that she'd not wanted her. Taylor thought that was what had hurt her the most that her mom had had no use for her until she got old enough to do her bidding. All her life, she'd done what she'd thought was the way things were supposed to go, and now it was as if someone was slapping her in the face for all the things that she had tried to do to make her mother happy. Standing up, she was surprised when every one of the Tuckers with her had stood as well. She looked at the judge when he asked her if she was all right.

"I don't know that I am, thank you for asking." She looked at her mom and then at her grandma. "I'm going home, sir. My attorney has all the paperwork that is necessary for you to understand what is really going on with my mom." He asked her if she wanted to change anything to make sure that information was correct. "No, sir. I believe that if I stay here much longer I'm going to hate my mother and right now I don't like her all that much but I don't hate her. Yet. The things that she's…well, I'm going home. Ivy, Mrs. Tucker will make sure I have the information that I need."

She was headed to the door when she stopped suddenly. She was never so happy to see Jack with her as she was at that moment. Smiling at him, she kissed him on the mouth and turned to look at her mother.

"I'm married to this wonderful man, Gilda Jane and as soon as it's possible, I'm going to have his children. Hundreds of them if he's willing." Her mother stood up and demanded that she take that back. With children, she told her there would be no time for her. "You're right. I don't care if I ever spend another minute with you for as long as I live."

Chapter 6

Emma backed her trailer up to the bay doors and waited for the signal that her locks were in place. Once they were, she put her truck into park and turned it off. Getting out, she had her gloves on and was ready to lock things in place when her mom said her name. She told her that she had a phone call.

"Take a message, and I'll call them back. We're behind enough on this load, and I want to get out of here as soon as they get me empty." Mom said that she'd do that and Emma finished up her locking down the trailer so that the people on the inside could work on getting things done. She hated to unload or load at this center.

This was the third time this month that their scheduled time had been put back. The first time, it had been only an hour. This time, it was nearly seven. She didn't have time to pussy foot around with a center if they didn't get their shit together. It was nearly dark when she decided to get into her bed and eat something with her mom. They'd been traveling together since her dad died five years ago, and it had been working out well for the two of them.

"What is it you've made us?" Mom handed her a plate of still steaming food of spaghetti and meatballs with garlic bread. "This is a bit much, don't you think?"

"Well, we had plans to have dinner out tonight, and I had my heart set on Italian. But this place has screwed that all up. Again. Besides, it's not that much to throw some frozen meatballs into the pot with the noodles. Not all that good but rib-sticking." They ate in silence for a few minutes before her mom spoke again. "I heard from your grandpa. He said that the real estate agent showed the house to a couple today. I hope they can sell it. I'm sick of paying taxes on the place when we don't even live there."

Her father had passed away a month and a half after the house had been completely paid off. Even with the mortgage that he'd borrowed against the house for her semi was now fully paid. From the beginning, her parents had supported her and now that she was free of any kind of payments to the bank, it made the profit that she made go a bit further when paying bills. The house being sold would save them a bit more. The two of them were making a profit now but without the monthly taxes, it would be easier to bank more.

"Don't forget to call that person back. I think that it was the same person as before, Denver Tucker." She said she'd call him as soon as she was finished eating. "Are they the ones that I sent all that paperwork to when they were looking for full-time drivers?"

"Yes. They're opening a distribution center along the coast. It'll be nice to be able to be at home at night. I know we'd have to buy us a place but it won't have to be as big as the place we had back home." The house had been in their family for generations, but neither she nor her mom were all that sentimental about the place. In fact, they both hated living there after her dad had died. "Maybe we can get us a little condo that has a couple of bedrooms, so we don't have to do yard crap either."

"I'd like to have a crafting room. And a big kitchen. Well, not big, but big enough that I could cook some cookies when I want." They had talked about this before, finding a driving job so that she could be home nightly. Her mom had gotten her driver's license to drive one of the big rigs but she didn't care for it. It had helped a great deal, her knowing how to drive to keep them on track when working. "You know how much it would cost to get us something smaller to go to the store in. I don't care for driving this sucker to the grocery store when we need something."

The two of them joked around about what they wanted in a house. Mom had said that she wanted a garden so that she could grow her own vegetables. Emma had wanted a garage to hold her rig in. She didn't care if it spent all its time in the weather. They only had nice weather down here where they were working for the most part.

After getting the dishes cleaned up—her mom used regular plates so as not to add to the amount of trash in the world, and it worked out great for them. The two of them only drank bottled water, so there were a lot of empty bottles in the rig when they got to a place to recycle them. Emma thought that the two of them worked well together. After checking to see how much longer they were going to be at this center, she called Denver Tucker.

"We've gone over your application, Ms. Holden, and it looks like we can work well together. I know you said that your mom didn't want to drive the bigger trucks but we do have cargo vans that she could drive that would bring in some good money for her as well." She told him that her mom would like that so long as it wasn't full-time. "I understand that she wants to work part-time, and any time that she can give us will be a blessing. The stores that we're suppling to are smaller stores that families run. But there are approximately seventy of them along the coast that we'll supply."

"That'll be wonderful." He told her that the center was nearly finished on the outside, but the inside was being worked on now. "There will be forty bay doors along with an entire section devoted to the perishable things that will be delivered, such as candy and drinks that can't handle the heat."

"The place we're at now has over a hundred bay doors, but they only use about twenty, which is what makes me late in and out of here. I don't know that they have enough people or they just don't care about times but it's a pain to be here." She shut down her talking about the center that she was working at. That didn't bode well to do that to a new employer. "Mom and I will be looking for a place to stay here too. About where the center is so that we can be halfway between each delivery."

"There are several condos that you can look

into. I can set up a realtor to help you out with that if you want. Also, you will be given an allowance when you have to stay over for whatever reason." She said that she understood there would be times for her to work overnight. "Good. I'm glad that we're on the same page. As for a starting date, it will be three weeks before the center starts taking in product. Most of the shelves have been put together and are standing. The merge area—the area where all the boxes and products are put on lines to head to the trucks has been running for a few days now, working out the bugs or whatever."

"Three weeks? That's a good deal faster than I thought." He asked her if she was coming to town this week to sign off on paperwork for her new job. "I really thought it would be months yet. I guess you guys know how to get people fired up."

"Yes, it seems that once the land was ready, the rest of it just fell into place. For now we're only distributing the things for Carol's Plaza but might branch out to other stores and shops as we get used to what we're doing. Of course, it helps that we have good drivers like you and your mom on our team, too." She thanked him, embarrassed that he'd say something like that. "If you don't have a return trip, we can have dinner tomorrow night. I understand that you only have one more week to go with the company you—"

"I don't work for a company, Mr. Tucker. I'm an independent driver. Working with you will be under contract, but I work because I want to, not because of someone ordering me to. I'm sorry if that makes a difference to you but that's what I wanted when I filled out the application to deliver for you and your company." He said that he'd known that but had forgotten. "Thank you. I don't want any misunderstanding going on between us."

"You're right. And neither do we. Thank you very much for reminding me." She told him that she was all right with it, and they moved on. She didn't want to have to only work for one firm. Especially for one that was just starting out. It could mean that she'd not be able to find employment if the company fell through on their promises and she sort of like having three meals a day and her truck. "What do you think about having dinner with my family. I will warn you there are a lot of us, but I think you can hold your own."

She wasn't so sure about that. Emma and her mom had been traveling together for years and had been their only company. But she agreed to have dinner with the family on Friday night. That gave her three days to get something to wear and hang out at the rest stop for truckers. A long hot shower was going to be on her list of things to get done. What she wouldn't give for a nice big bathtub right now, she thought with a smile.

After leaving the center, they headed to the store. They'd not stopped for supplies in a while so they were about out of everything. In the bed area, they had a microwave, a small oven as well as a good-sized refrigerator. All the comforts of home and none of the work that went along with it. Her mom was in charge of the area where she cooked, and the two of them had gotten used to sharing a bed when there was time for them to get a good night's sleep. They got along well and had a wonderful time seeing the country. At least this end of the country.

"What do you think about going to see a movie tomorrow night?" Mom looked shocked that she'd ask such a question. "It's all right if you don't want to go, Mom. It was just something that I thought you'd enjoy that was about as normal as two people can get."

"How about dinner, too? Oh, it would be nice to have time for both, don't you think?"

She told her that she owed her a meal anyway. "I would love to have a date tomorrow night. That'll give us a little bit of time to catch up on things that have been going on. I know how much you dislike having the radio on, but there are newspapers that we can look at, too."

Her mom was teasing her, but she'd been right in saying that she didn't like the radio on. It wasn't just the bad news that seemed to be on every station but she really did enjoy her quiet time. They would listen to a book if they'd find one that they both thought that they'd enjoy but other than that, the radio was never on.

Picking up some laundry detergent and some softener, she was going to spend tomorrow morning at the laundry mat to get some things cleaned up. They didn't really wear all that much in clothing, the usual things really but since they rarely got out of the rig more than a couple of times a week, neither of them saw any reason to put on clean clothing daily.

While she was doing laundry the next morning, she took her mom's advice and picked up the local and larger city newspaper. It had been a lot harder than she thought it should have been to pick up actual papers, but she managed to find a couple. Mostly, it was the local stuff that she read, but other things were going on around town, too, that she was interested in. Like talk of the charity Tucker Charities.

It went on to tell how the Tucker family, along with the Fosters, had set up the charity to help people get back up on their feet. Not just individuals but also companies that wanted to expand and or start-up. Like the distribution center that she was going to be working for.

It was going to hire as many as six hundred people. All the work on the building was done by locals when it could be done, and once it was up to full capacity, including truckers like herself, there would be over a thousand new jobs. She wholly believed in the trickle-down theory in that if there were that many jobs, people from all other walks of life would benefit from it as well, like restaurants and especially schools. Her mom came into the laundry mat just as she was putting the last load in the dryer and showed her the haircut she'd gotten.

"I nearly fell asleep while she was washing my hair. It's nice to be pampered a bit, don't you think?" She told her mom that she didn't care for people touching her. "Yes, I remember that. You were always an odd man out. But I love you, and that's all that matters."

Her mom took the papers with her and said she'd be in the rig. As she was taking out her pants from the dryer, she noticed that there wasn't much going on in the place. Not that she knew all that much about laundry mats, she just thought that there would be more people in the place on a Thursday morning.

It took her two trips to get her things out to the rig and by the time they'd gotten things put away and the things hung up that didn't go in the dryer, they were ready for some dinner. Ordering a pizza sounded good to her but her mom wanted to sit someplace that was larger than a table. In the shopping center where they were, two shops served pizza, and they decided on which one to go to after flipping a coin. If only life were that easy, as just a flip of a quarter could make the decision for life's little things.

"I'm stuffed." Emma looked around the room and noticed a man at the counter talking to the cashier. She wondered if he had wanted something to eat and didn't have the money when he turned suddenly and looked at her. She didn't move, there was something so very strange about the look he was giving her. "Mom, it's time we get back."

They were gathering up their things when the man came to their table. He didn't say anything but continued to stare at her. Finally having enough, she shoved him hard enough for him to hit the floor and stepped around him. Just as she was taking a step toward the door, he grabbed her leg and had her falling on her ass.

Turning around, she grabbed him by the arm and twisted. The sound of something snapping in his arm didn't make her feel any better, but she was free of him and stood up. Whatever was wrong with the man, she wanted nothing to do with him. As she was getting up, he came at her again, this time with a knife in his hand that had been on their table.

"Back off." She didn't want to have to pull out her gun, but her mom had no such trouble. Putting it to the back of his head, telling him to drop the knife, she was able to limp her way away from him.

Whatever was going on in the man's head, she didn't want to hang around and find out. As is was now, she was beginning to feel the pain of being tossed around and didn't much care for it.

Mom had the man on the floor with his

hands behind his head when the police arrived. While she didn't know what his problem had been with her, he was pissed off enough for the police to take him away almost as soon as they arrived. Sitting down hard on the chair that had been right behind her, she felt something warm and wet running down the back of her head. Turning to look at her mom, she yelled at the girl behind the counter to call an ambulance. That was the last thing she remembered as the floor simply came up from beneath her feet and slapped her out. Christ, all she'd wanted was a few slices of hot pizza, and now she was going to have to explain why she wasn't going to be able to have dinner with her new bosses.

~*~

"They didn't say what the man was going to do to her. Please don't ask me that again, Denver. I might have to wrestle with you a bit before we get to the hospital." He laughed, and Bailee glared at him. "I'm serious. Her mother said that the man just came at them—well, Emma, at least and knocked her around. If not for her being armed, there is no telling what might have happened to her. Did you know that Emma's mom was a former cop? That's good to know."

"I didn't know, no. But I'm glad for it." They were pulling into the emergency department parking lot an hour after hearing from Charlotte Holden. "I'm so glad that she called us. It's a shame that this happened, but I'm sure that we can get to the bottom of this soon."

"I wouldn't be so sure. He seemed sort of deranged, according to Charlotte. I'm betting that he saw her as a target or something and was going to simply rob her." Denver asked why he'd pick her. "I don't know. Perhaps because she's beautiful. Also, being a redhead makes me think that he believes all those stories about redheads being magical or something. I've even heard that some people think that they're evil and in league with the devil himself."

"I'd heard that too." They were shown to the room where Emma was but the room was empty of a bed when they arrived. Ms. Holden was there, sitting on one of the chairs, crying. It was her that got the woman to stop crying and to tell her what was going on.

"The man had a picture on him that showed a red-headed woman that sort of looked like Emma. She had fuller lips than my daughter and seemed to be a bit heavier. But he thought that she was the woman at the welfare office who had taken his kids away from him. He was set to kill her so that he'd not have to face her in court. If he acts like that around his children, I'm glad they were taken from him. The man was set to kill my little girl." Bailee was sorry that it had come to this but she told the other woman that she was glad that she remembered to call them. "That was Emma. She woke up a couple of times and told me to call you guys to explain why we might not make it to your house tomorrow night. We were having such a good day too when the man attacked us. The man that runs the shop we were in seemed to not understand me telling him to get the police until I had to smack him a good one. I hated to do it, but he was just standing there while Emma was bleeding on the floor."

"I would have been terrified if that had happened to me. Especially with it being my child." Denver asked where Emma was. "Oh yes, I should have asked that first thing. I'm sorry."

"It's fine. She was taken for a CAT scan of her head and neck. They haven't put any stitches in her yet. I think they were waiting for the tests to come back. I'm going to have to call someone to get the rig taken care of. The shopping center has a strict rule about leaving rigs on their lot overnight."

"I'll make a couple of phone calls, and it will be all right. Once we figure out what's going on here, I'll have someone drive it to our house, so you don't have to worry about it." Charlotte thanked them both. "Do you need anything, ma'am?"

"Just my girl to be all right." Bailee sat with her while Denver went to make the phone calls. It really wasn't that big of a deal to have it moved, but there was no point in leaving it out there to be vandalized. "I just wish we'd have eaten in the rig if it was going to cause all that much trouble."

Before she could say anything, Emma was brought into the room. She looked a little out of it, and the nurse explained that the doctor had said she could have something for the pain. Whatever it was, it looked like it was doing the trick for her.

"They're going to keep her overnight. Just to make sure that she's here to get some meds when she needs them." Bailee wondered what would have happened to her if they were to have released her since she and her mom both lived in their rig. She was going to make arrangements to have Charlotte stay with them and Emma when she got out of the hospital. It was the only way that they were going to get some rest, she thought. "Once the doctor looks over the scans, then we'll come in and put some stitches in her head. It's a good-sized cut but shouldn't put her down for very long."

After explaining that she was a red head and would need a bit more to knock her out, the nurse laughed and said that the doctor had a red-headed wife and knew how that was true. After she left, Charlotte went to the bed and held onto Emma's hand. Bailee felt her eyes fill with tears. After so many things going on with mothers lately, it was nice to see a family get along so well.

"Emma is my step-daughter. When her father met me, she was about two at the time. We dated for a while, and Emma and I became close to each other. Then, when her dad died suddenly, we were all each other had." She told her she was sorry. "I am as well. We didn't have a lot of time together, Frank and I, but we certainly loved this little girl. She's done so much for me that I don't know that I would have made it without her bullying me all the time. In a good way, you understand."

"Yes, of course. She told me how you bullied her at times as well. The two of you are good together." She said that they had to be because they were in cramped quarters all the time. "Yes,

I can see how that would make a difference in a relationship. I don't know that I could have been in a rig for as long as the two of you have been."

"Like I said, it was for the best." Charlotte looked at Emma. "We, the two of us, have sold off everything that we owned to make this work for us. I wanted to see the country and she wanted to drive so that she was her own boss. I have no idea how much longer she plans to do this, but I've never been so proud of anyone as I am of her. We have a bit of a savings account thanks to her and we're doing something that very few mother and daughters get to do with each other."

"I would imagine that you two are the exception to the rule about families getting along so well. Taylor, you'll meet her later. She's having issues with her mom right now. I heard from the courthouse that she's been arrested for threatening a sitting judge, along with a few other things that are going to get her jail time. Now that woman is a nutball." The two of them talked for a while, waiting for someone to come in and talk to them. Denver came back to tell them that the rig had been taken care of, and she could tell that Charlotte was relieved about that. She had looked it up earlier and couldn't believe the cost of a simple rig. And theirs had extra stuff in it for them to live.

It was nearly midnight when they admitted Emma. She didn't want to stay, but her mom said she'd feel better if she had. That was when she told them that their house was open for them and that they'd be proud to have them staying with them until she felt better. She had a feeling that the only reason that Emma agreed was because her mom did so quickly. It was lovely to see such a bond between two people like she was.

After setting up Charlotte in one of the guest rooms, she and Denver went to bed, too. Tomorrow was going to be a long day as they had meetings all day with different vendors that wanted to come to the town. She was excited and scared at the same time. So many people were depending on them for new jobs and businesses coming in that it made her slightly nervous, too.

The next morning, Charlotte heard from Emma about when she was going to be discharged. The rig had been brought to the house and she was happy to see that Charlotte was able to get herself some clean clothing. It was wonderful, too, that she got to see a first-hand look at the inside of the little home they'd been living in for the past five years.

"I don't think that I could have done it." Bailee thought about some of the magic that was in the family and wondered if they could tweak the rig a bit so that they had a lot more room. That was a question for later, she thought. She wanted to make sure that everything else turned out fine for the two women before the center was finished.

Several hours after having her breakfast, Bailee was ready to face the meetings that she had set up. Off and on, she would check on Emma, but for the most part she was glad to be getting these meetings done with. She'd know better than to have them all on the same day again. It was trying for her to have to keep straight what each meeting was about. She felt like she was in a tennis match with things going back and forth.

However, at the end of the day, it was a great accomplishment to know that seven more businesses were coming to town that would hire two hundred people. Next week, they were going to do the groundbreaking for the parts place for wine barrels being made right here in their little town.

Dever was picking up something for dinner as they both had had a fulfilling day. Emma was in the living room relaxing and her mom was on the phone with someone. Once she left the room, Bailee asked her how she was doing. She could tell that she was in a bit of pain, but she said it was nice to be settled someplace other than a hospital bed.

"I would imagine. And something bigger than the bed that you two share." She said that there was that as well. "I'm hoping that you guys live close enough that we can get together sometimes. I fell in love with your mom, and she's having a good time house-hunting with the realtor."

"She's going to be spending the most time in the place so it might as well be her that finds us something. I think she's finished with traveling now and wants to settle in one place." She nodded and then said that she'd spoken to her a bit. "Not that I'd turn her down if she wanted to go with me at times. Being home at night has been the most appealing thing you offered us. Mom wants to put in a little garden and have a place where she could sit and read. I'm betting that we won't even own a television set when we get someplace. We've enjoyed the peace and quiet for too long for us to go back to wanting all that noise again.

"I can understand that as well. I was going to ask you, do you still feel up to having dinner with us all tomorrow night? I don't want to make you do anything that you don't want to do." She said other than a pounding headache, she felt pretty good. "Good. I was going to cancel if you thought you couldn't do it. I can't wait to get this project, along with a few more, started. It's going to be so good for the area."

There was more to it than that but she didn't mention it just yet. Bailee was thinking that it would be wonderful if it turned out that Emma was one of the others mates. However, since she wanted it to happen, it wouldn't. But time would tell, she supposed. Tomorrow was going to be another long and scary day with all the meetings that she had coming up.

Chapter 7

Gilda was about as pissed off as she'd been in a long time. Not only was she mad at her daughter, but the entire world seemed to be against her. Now here she sat in the jail with nothing to do. All she'd wanted to do was to make sure that her daughter would take care of her for the rest of her life and she wouldn't do it.

Then there were the children. She knew for a fact that children were time-consuming. She'd never been so glad to have Henriette out of the picture soon. The old bat couldn't be around much longer. The fact that she'd been around this long boggled her mind. Why couldn't she just die like the rest of the old people did? Who knew. She was probably making a deal with the devil, and that's why she was still around. No matter how much she wanted the old bat dead, she just wouldn't die.

"You have a visitor. Would you like to have them come back here, or would you like to go to the conference room?" She said that she wanted out of there. "That's not what I asked you. Where did you want to have this meeting?"

"Who is it?" When he didn't answer her, she wanted to get out of this place and beat the shit out of him. It was bad enough that they never got close enough to her to allow her to touch them. "I'll meet them in the conference room, I guess. But if it's someone that I don't want to meet with, then you'll have to take me right back."

He didn't say anything but for her to back against the far wall. It was all she could do not to slam his head against the bars and be done with him. But that would be too much work, and she didn't have it in her to make herself do anything that someone else should do for her.

Her daughter was in the room when she was brought in. After they actually chained her to the table and her legs to the hook on the floor, the cop stood against the far wall and waited. She told him three times that he needed to leave them alone, but all he did was put his hand on his gun and tell her to get on with it.

"I suppose you came in here to get me out of here. I'm not so sure how I feel about being around you after all you've done to me." Taylor asked her what she was talking about. "What are you doing to get me out of here? I'm hoping that you know, too, that I'm not going to put up with the crappy way you've been treating me, Taylor. I demand that you do as you're told and make my life better."

"Your life is just the way that it should be." She snorted and didn't say anything else. "There are some things that you missed when you were in the courthouse that I'm here to explain to you now. First of all, it's the money. I've given you the money from the insurance policy that was Dad's. You've already spent it all, but I'm being generous today. Also, as per your request, there is no more money going out of your accounts, such as payments due on your house or any kind of stock prices. You only have the cash that I'm giving you."

"Good. And there won't be any more of it going out for investments either, correct?" She explained to her that without investments, her money could soon be gone. "You'll just give me more. That's the way that I want it."

"No. If you want more money, you're going to have to work for it. Every penny that I've made is all mine. I have investments as well as projects that are going to be making me a great deal more money." Gilda asked her about living arrangements. "You're going to be spending time in jail for threatening the judge, but other than that, I have no idea what's going to happen to you. And frankly I could care less what happens to you from now on. I'm finished with you and your demands, too."

"We'll just see about that, won't we? Where will I be living? Don't think that I didn't notice that you didn't answer me." She told her. "I need to live with you and only you. I'll not have that man around where he takes attention from me. You'll have to get rid of him and that's final. I won't have you having children either. They're nothing but soul suckers, and I want your attention on me."

"That's too bad." Had she not been chained up, she might well have slapped her like she used to do when she was a child and back-talked her. "You'll have the condo that you lived in before this and someone will come in twice a week to clean up. That doesn't mean that she'll be cooking or doing your laundry. There will only be a light cleaning. If you make a huge mess like I know that you do, then that will be on you to clean it up."

"No. No, that's not going to work for me. You'll have to pay for her to keep my house tidy. And speaking of which, I want a place that is bigger than yours. You'll live with me so that I know that you're paying your full attention to me. No more dates and working days. I'll not have you too worn out to do the things that I want." Taylor just stared at her. "Did you hear me? You should be writing things down so that I don't have to repeat myself when I'm free of here. Which had better be soon. I don't like it here. They won't do as I say, and it makes me upset. You don't want me upset, do you, darling?"

"I'm not your darling. I'm your daughter who—have you always been this selfish and demanding? I'm sure that I know the answer to that but I'd like to hear it from you? Why do you think that everything is about you?" Gilda asked her what she was talking about. "These demands and rules. You have to know that I'm not going to be following any of them. You're lucky that I've given you the things that I have. And like I said, after you've run through your money, I will not be giving you any more."

"Yes, you will. You don't want me to have to suffer to be without things. I know better. It's your duty as my child that you keep me happy and without any kind of stress. And anything that you think you want to do is stressful for me so you'll not do that. Anything that I don't give you permission for Taylor isn't going to work for me. So just get those thoughts right out of your head." Taylor just stared at her. "Do you hear me, or do I need to go over this once more? I'm serious when I tell you that if you have any plans of dating, getting married, or—and this one will get you in serious hurt, there will be no children. I was lucky in you that you were my only child. I know how demanding you can be, and I won't have it. Do you understand what I'm saying to you? No children. No men and certainly nothing to do with that man that you think you might marry."

"We *are* married." She told her that she would just have to get a divorce. "No, I'm not. I love him, and he loves me. That's the way it's going to be from now on. Also, while I'm going over things that you want. Unless you can afford a bigger condo or home, you'll be paying for it. You can live rent-free in the one that you're in because I own it. Otherwise, you're going to have to deal with things on your own. I won't be spending any time with you and certainly not living with you. I have my own life now and I plan on living the way that I want to. In fact, Jack and I have made arrangements to live with Grandma in her home.

It's large enough for the three of us, and there will be plenty of room when the children—which is going to happen—come along."

"You'll do no such thing." Gilda turned to the cop. "Undo me so that I can slap some sense into her head. She's getting out of hand, and as her mother, I demand that you allow me to be free enough to knock some sense into her. To think that she thinks that—there will be no life for you, Taylor, unless I say so. Do you understand me? I rule you because I had to have you. But no more of you thinking that you can have a life of your own. You will do what I said and I'll not hear another word out of you. Where do you think you're going? I'm not nearly finished with my demands."

"I'm finished with you." Taylor gathered up her things and she started for the door. "This is the last time that I'm coming to see you. Calling the number that you had will no longer work for you. The police station has been told that they're not to call us for any more of your demands. When, and I doubt that it will be anytime soon, you get out, you'll do as you wish, and I'll not have a thing to do with you. Do you understand me?"

"You're going to take care of me, Taylor. I swear to you. I don't want to have to show you

my angry side if you keep saying things like this."
Taylor said that she wasn't afraid. "You had better
be. I'm not going to allow you to toss me aside as
if I'm nothing to you. Your grandparents did that,
and I won't allow that to happen to me again. I
deserve the best, and you will provide it for me."

"You go on thinking that." She was out the
door before she could remind her about getting
her out of the cell she was in. If, and she still didn't
understand why she had to be in jail, but if she had
to stay here, then she should have the nicest and
biggest cell along with things that weren't so hard
and drab. Taylor should be making sure that she's
pampered even in jail. It was something that she
had thought to talk to her about.

Being taken back to her cell, she noticed that
someone had been inside. Her sheets were gone
that had been lying at the bottom of the bed as well
as there were clean towels for her to use when she
showered. So far she had managed to avoid taking
a shower with the other people in the place. And
as far as her sheets being there for her to make her
bed, she wasn't going to do that either. She could,
she supposed but so long as she had breath in her
body, someone was going to do it for her. It was
the least that they could do for her being Gilda

Jane. People needed to get on board with how to treat her.

It's not like she wanted all the money in the world. Just enough that when she wanted to go shopping she didn't have to worry over credit cards and the like. Gilda didn't think it was all that big of a deal that people were to wait on her, either. She wouldn't be mean to them. Demanding things to be her way after she gave them the rules but they needed to be on the same page as she was about how she should be treated. People should want to take care of her all the time. She was a nice person, and people should understand that as well.

Taylor should know by now the rules about her life. She'd been taking care of her needs since she'd been a little girl. Training her hadn't been that much of a hardship. A few slaps here and there when she thought that she could think beyond caring for her, and Taylor straightened right up. It was all because of that woman, Henriette. Why she was still alive was beyond her.

"She should have died decades ago. Where does she get off living to be nearly a hundred years old and pampering to every need of Taylor? The stupid old woman was going to feel the back of her hand when she saw her again. The old bat had said something to Taylor that made her not want to help her.

Gilda would admit that she was needy. She didn't have to be. But she also didn't like doing things for herself. She didn't care not to be the center of attention either. Everyone and everything should be about her and no one else. She remembered a baby shower that had been had for her when she was huge with Taylor. Henry Paul asked her if she was enjoying herself.

"No. Everything that they've brought to my party is for the kid. Why? It's not like I'm going to put anything that is pretty on her. That would draw the attention from me to even have to be around her when she's dressed up in some of the outfits that they brought for her. And how come no one thought to bring me something? I would have loved a nice new dress or two. Some pretty shoes. No, all the attention is on this kid and not me. How could you allow them to do that to me, Henry Paul?"

He just walked away from her. He'd done that a great deal in the later part of their marriage. Then, when she found out that she was going to have a baby, he did treat her a lot differently. She thought about something else then. Sex.

She enjoyed it to a point, but when she came, that's what it was called, she didn't want another thing to do with Henry Paul and his dick. He tried to explain to her that he needed his release, too, but she didn't care about his needs.

It was hers that she wanted that had nothing to do with him. What did she care about his needs anyway? Gilda had allowed him to touch her with it, didn't she? She thought him to be selfish about sex anyway. Why did he have to touch her all over the place when all she wanted was to come. Shivering, she thought of the one time he tried to have her suck on his cock. It still made her gag when she thought of putting that nasty thing in her mouth. Christ, men were so stupid about sex, she told herself.

Pacing her cell, one of the officers came back to speak to her. The first thing out of his mouth was that she needed to make her bunk up. She told him that when the person who had mopped the room had left them there, they should have made up the bed, too. It wasn't her job to do housekeeping just because they had put her behind bars for no reason.

"You're going to see the judge in the

morning. We'll leave here at seven and arrive at the courthouse at seven-thirty." She told him that it was too early for her to get up and that they'd have to do it later in the day. "He's not going to wait around for you to have your shit together, Ms. Murphy. You'll follow the rules like the rest of the inmates. Your hearing will be called fourth, and you'll need to have your attorney present."

"I don't have an attorney. I've said this to you before. I don't need one because I've done nothing wrong. And if I'm going to be called before him fourth, why do I have to go so early? That's the stupidest thing that I've ever heard. Making me get up early so that I can wait on his ass all morning? No. You'll make arrangements to come back and get me when my time is ready." He just went on about how things were going to work as if she didn't say a word. "I'm not going to be getting ready then. As I have said, I don't need to be there at that god-awful hour, so you can just make arrangements to help me out. That's the least you can do."

"The least I can do is whatever I told you. It's going to be up at six-thirty, leave by seven to be there at seven-thirty. That is what is going to happen. If you're not up and ready to go, then

I'll drag your ass out so that I'm on time with my duties. That is the way that it's going to be." She'd just see about that. Where was her daughter to pay off people when she needed her to? "Lights out at ten tonight because of the early hour."

"We'll just see about that," she said aloud this time. "You people are not being very nice to me, and I'm going to have to go over your heads to get you to pay attention when I speak."

Gilda was sitting on the side of her cot when the entire room went black. Not even the moon could penetrate the darkness, and she hated it. The black of night had never been anything that she cared for, and right now, it was ten times worse. She didn't have her little nightlight to guide the way in the event she woke to use the bathroom. Fucking people.

~*~

Taylor was about as needy as she'd ever been. Working the lines at the new building just to see if the scanner was working well nearly had her sobbing in pain with her need so high. As soon as she found Jack, she was going to strip him down and take him on the first hard place, even if it was the dining room table, and have her way with him. This was his fault because he'd not been in bed when she'd woke this morning, and she'd been needing him all day.

"I'm nearly a mile from where you are, and I can feel you. What are you doing that has you so worked up?" She told him that she needed him. "And I you, my love, but I told you I had to go to the fish market first thing this morning. You told me that you'd be right as rain. I take it that you're not."

"No, I'm not all right. What did you do to me before you left? I've never in all my life, especially not with you around have I ever felt like I'm being strummed like a guitar string." He told her that he loved that saying. "Love it or not, Jack Anderson Tucker, I'm going to jump your bones as soon as I get home with you."

For the rest of the afternoon, she began setting up the office that she would use while there. With the way things were going in the distribution center, it would only be a couple of more weeks before it was up and running. Not really. There was still a great deal of work on the inside that needed to be done, but it was going much better than she had expected.

By the time she got home, she was exhausted. She had long since decided that her libido was doing her more harm than good, so she made sure that she thought of anything other than sex. As it was right now, she didn't think that she could have gotten wet with the way that her body was reacting to her day. It had been a long fourteen-hour shift, and she was ready for bed. Jack was waiting in the front hall when she got to the house.

"No one is here. It's the cook's night off." She nodded, her body trying to catch up with his body. When he dropped to his knees in front of her, she nearly got down as well, but when he pulled her body to his mouth, Taylor nearly cried out. Never had he done anything like this before, and she was excited to try it.

Once he stripped off her clothing from the waist down, she was wet, dripping down her thighs wet just for him. Pulling her body to his mouth, crying out, she knew that she was going to come almost as soon as he touched her. Jack was ever so good at making her come right away.

He ate at her over and over until she was weak with it. Her first climax nearly had her tumble over on top of him, and the second and third had her trembling. Begging him to stop only made him work harder until she finally had to pull him from her by yanking his hair and staring at him.

"You're killing me." He grinned at her and leaned in to suckle at her clit again. The short yet powerful release had her whimpering for not just more, but some of her wanted him to stop as well. When he stood up, she had to hold onto him.

"I'm going to enjoy this. As many times as I can." Jack backed her up until she felt the table behind her touch her back. He lifted her up and, sat her on the table and moved between her thighs. His cock slowly entered her until she thought she'd die from the pleasure.

"Jack, I love you." Tearing at the rest of her clothing, she was naked before him. He had, at some point, pulled open his jeans and taken off his shirt. It was almost too much for her. His body had her wanting things from him that she knew he'd give her.

When he moved to her breast and suckled on the tip before pulling the heavy flesh into his mouth. His tongue moved over the nipple over and over as he entered her deeper and then deeper still. When he was as deep as he could go, he looked at her.

"You're so hot, my love. And wet. You've been thinking of this, haven't you?" He rolled his hips, and she could swear he was at the back of her throat. "Come for me. Tighten that pretty pussy around me and come."

Jack had never talked to her this way before. They hadn't been together for that long, so she rarely thought of anything other than sex anymore. But this man, this man who had been away from her all day, was making her think of things she'd never thought of before.

"I want to take you into my mouth." He groaned and rolled his hips again. "I want to taste you too, feel you fucking my mouth."

"You're going to make me come too soon if you keep that up." Taylor rolled her own hips and watched his face. His fingers on her hips tightened, and she knew that he was close.

Wrapping her ankles around him, she sat up and took his mouth. His body started to move in and out of her faster now, and she felt her climax rolling along her body. When he nipped at her throat, Taylor threw back her head and cried out at her release.

His body exploded in hers even as she felt his mouth bite down hard enough at her throat to draw blood. Her next climax had her seeing stars. His own roar of completion made her feel like she could take on the world. Holding onto him, she felt her love for him warm her entire body. Then she closed her eyes and didn't remember another thing about anything at all.

Looking at the clock, she realized that she'd slept the entire night without waking. Usually, she would have to get up at least once to go to the bathroom, but she must have been more tired than she'd thought. Taking a long hot shower, rubbing her sponge hard into her tight muscles, she was feeling good about herself and her ability to get around. Getting dressed, her favorite part of the magic that she'd gotten, Taylor made her way to the kitchen to see if she could get herself a late breakfast or an early lunch. Either one would have satisfied her about now.

After having a couple of glasses of fresh juice, two eggs, and some biscuits, she was ready to hit the day running. She hadn't thought of her mother in the last few hours, but the thought of her going to court this morning made her wish that she could have snuck in and seen how it was going. She could probably go, she thought, but she was having such a nice day that she didn't want to fuck it up by trying to get into the courthouse with her mom. She had plenty of things to do today.

At nearly three in the afternoon, she'd gone

over fifty applications for employment for the new center. They were going to need four times that many to just start out but she knew too that she had plenty of time yet. Getting someone in who could do the daily things would help her out, so that, for now anyway, was what she was looking for. Looking up when someone said her name, she was beyond thrilled to see her grandma there.

"I was just at my doctor, and I'm officially cancer-free. I know that I was told that, but to hear it from the man who told me I only had weeks to go makes me feel like I should be rubbing it into his face from now until eternity." They both laughed. "I was feeling so good that I went to the courthouse—staying in the back, of course, to listen to what was going on with Gilda. My goodness, child, she sure is upset with you."

"I almost went myself, but I didn't want to hear her yelling at me to make things right for her." Grandma told her that she wasn't going to be getting out of jail anytime too soon. "What's she done now? Not that I should be surprised. Nothing about my mother surprises me anymore. I wonder how her parents and my dad put up with her."

"She told the judge that she was going to kill him when she was freed. That didn't sit too well with him, if you can imagine." She agreed with her grandma. "She also said that she was going to kill Jack, not that she had his name right because you two were fornicating, and that was going to piss her off if there was a child from it. Gilda even hinted that if there was a child, she was going to make sure that you didn't get to have it as well."

"I never realized how sick she was. I mean, I've been caring for her most of my life and I didn't even see it. Not until the last few months. I think you taking me into your home has made my eyes open a great deal more." Grandma told her that she wanted to talk to her and Jack about the house. "No. I'm not going to have you kicked to the curb because you think that house is just right for us. Jack and I have talked it over, and if you don't live here with us, we're going to move out as well and sell the place off. It wouldn't be the same without you around. I need you in my life, Grandma, and I don't want to have to hunt you down to find you so that I can have lunch or talk to you."

"It really is a large house, honey." She told her it was, and that was all they were going to talk about. "You're stubborn. Just like your grandfather used to be. He'd be like...when he wanted things to be done a certain way, he'd drive you to the moon and back until you say things his way. I miss him every day."

"I wish I could have gotten to know him. At least pictures of him with me. He seemed like a good man for you and this family." Grandma told her that Henry would never have been able to marry Gilda had he been around. "Then I'd not be born to have you around. No, I guess someone has to suffer a little so that things are just the way they are now. With the exception of my mom."

They both laughed again. It was wonderful knowing that her grandma was going to be around for a long time. Just being able to talk to her for a few minutes every day made her life so much better.

Chapter 8

He couldn't help but marvel at the sea this time of the year. Colby had finally gotten his first of four ships that he wanted and he couldn't be happier with the way things had turned out. The LouCinda, named in honor of his grandma, was booked up until the first of February. The other three ships would come as he could afford them. And from the way things were looking, it wouldn't be that long of a wait.

The two that were going to really test his abilities were the first one in a week that had five fishermen and the second one that was carrying eight. His brother Jack was going to help him out with the food and join him on the boat for a few days. It would be like old times.

Hanging out with family had always been his favorite thing to do. Especially when there were only a couple of them to do it with. Having nine brothers and sisters had made alone time nearly nonexistent growing up, so he was going to take it when he could get it. He'd have Jack all to himself for a few days, and they'd work on the ship together and then play around at night. He was glad that his new wife, Taylor, was all for it. He loved all his family, including the ones that had come to them through mates.

"Mr. Tucker? There's a landline call for you in the cabin." He and the crew that he'd hired were putting the finishing touches on the Lou to be ready in the event that someone wanted to go out today or tomorrow. Going into the living area, he picked up the phone and answered it.

"My name is David Sledge. I want to book your boat for the next three days." For whatever reason, Colby's lion wrapped around him as if to warn him of danger. "It'll only be for the three days, and I'm willing to pay double your rental fee if you could just let me and my crew have the boat for that amount of time."

"I'm sorry, I don't rent out my time like that." He said it would only be for three days. "I heard you, Mr. Sledge but I'm not in the habit of renting out something without my being on the ship as well. It's not the way that I do business." He said that he'd rent the boat but how about if it was just himself but with his own crew that went out. "Again, I don't work like that. I'm sorry. You'll have to keep looking. To be honest, Mr. Sledge, I don't know that there is anyone that rents out a boat without her captain and crew."

"You're just starting out, Mr. Tucker. How can you have those kinds of rules when you've not even taken out your first group?" Again, his lion wrapped tighter around him. The man knew that he was new and that was why he'd thought to get him to do what he wanted. "I mean, can you really turn down something like double your fees at this stage of the game? It's just for three days. Two and a half if you'd like. Come on, now. I'll triple your fees, and neither of us will be out much of anything."

"I said that I'm not going to rent out my boat to you, Mr. Sledge. Now, if there is nothing else, I've things to do." The man growled low, and that was when he realized that he might be in just a little bit of trouble here. Reaching out for Parker Foster, the grand witch of all witches. *"I'm in trouble here. Big time, I think."*

"The phone call?" He told her that was it, and she told him not to hang up. He knew that one of the Fosters, he was too nervous to remember their name, could touch a phone and know just who

was calling and where they were. Today, he just wanted not to be killed. Even if he couldn't, he didn't want to be hurt either. She told him that she had it.

"Listen here, buddy. You're going to rent me your boat, and you're not going to have one little bit of — Christ." When the line went dead, he gripped it harder to his face and sat down. If not for the chair being just behind him, Colby wasn't sure what he might have done. Landed on the floor for sure.

"*I have it taken care of, Colby, my friend.*" He thanked her and asked what he needed to do now. "*Just hang up the phone. He's not going to bother you again. This I promise you.*"

That sounded scary to him. Very much so. So, doing as she said, still, a little weak-kneed to do any walking, Colby sat at the desk and waited for her to come to him. He figured that she would, just to explain a little of what happened but he wasn't even sure he wanted any information right now. Just as he was getting up to do the rest of the work on the boat, Parker appeared in the room with him.

"You were smart to call someone to help you." He asked her if he'd wanted him to dump a body. "Smart man. Yes, that's exactly what he wanted from you. Mr. Sledge had two, as a matter of fact, that he needed to get rid of quickly. You're a smart man."

"I'm a terrified one, is what I am." She laughed, and so did he. "As soon as he wanted to rent my boat without my crew scared me enough to know that I was in over my head. Will that happen a lot, do you think? That someone will think they can just rent my boat for nefarious things?"

"Yes. You're new to the area and they figure that you have no experience with dealing with that sort of pushy person and that you'd cave when he got aggressive with you. Or that you're so desperate for money that you'll do just about anything to get a few bucks to keep you going. I'm going to make it so that you won't have that problem again. When men of his caliber are looking for a way to get out of a sticky situation call, they won't see your number anywhere." He thanked her. "You're so very welcome. Also, if something happens while you're out on a fishing trip, I'm going to give you a faerie to help. She'll be able to keep you apprised of anything that is going on from now on."

After Parker left, he felt a bit better. He'd

even remembered to ask her about the trips that he had booked and she told him he'd be just fine. Deciding that he needed to have some things on the boat to keep him and his crew safe, Colby got online and looked at things that they could use. He never thought of how far out in the water he would be with perfect strangers.

"*I have a couple of questions for you.*" He smiled when Jack contacted him. "*Do you have a menu that they can choose from? Like you know, lunch is sandwiches. Dinner will be three or four courses. Anything like that?*"

"*No. Though I think that sandwiches for lunch would be perfect. They can still enjoy fishing while eating. And smaller bags of chips to hold onto.*" They talked about having things easier to eat than what he'd have in his restaurant and then things to have for dinner. "*If the crew catches some of the fish, will you be able to serve those up as well?*"

It was great to be able to bounce ideas off of Jack, too. He was a smart person to go to when he had questions about food and serving things to his guests. The one thing that he'd been sure to go over with him was a drinks menu.

While there weren't going to be any drinks on his boat that he provided, a person could bring on some of their own so long as they signed a waiver saying that they were responsible for themselves if something were to go wrong when renting the crew and boat out. Also, he would provide the fishing gear for the trip. Again, so long as they signed a waiver if they were to bring their own, they were solely responsible for it.

There were other things that they discussed while talking, and when he realized it was coming up on six, Colby said that he had a date and needed to get ready for it. Of course, that got his brother to teasing him, and when he closed the connection, he was still smiling.

He knew this woman wasn't his mate. Colby had been out with her before. They were just fuck buddies. Each of them knew that nothing could ever be more than it was at that moment. Still, she was fun to have on his arm when he wanted a nice dinner and perhaps a play to go and see. No attachments were his favorite way to date.

Picking up Olivia at seven, they were headed to the restaurant when she told him about her job. She was a beat cop and enjoyed her job a great deal. There had been a murder-suicide happening today, and she was telling him how they'd found two frozen bodies in the place after the police were called. Colby nearly ran off the road when she mentioned frozen bodies.

"Are you all right?" He nodded, afraid that he might confess to something that he didn't have anything to do with. "You looked a little frightened there for a moment. Did you hear about it down at the docks?"

"No, I didn't hear about it. The radio was on. Maybe I heard something about it then. You know how much Randy loves to have his music blaring." She laughed and said she wondered if he could hear very well he liked it so loud. "So there was a man that killed someone, and you found the bodies in the freezer?"

"Something like that. The guy was a big-time thug that we've been trying to get for a few years. When the call came in about hearing gunshots, they sent someone to his residence and found four bodies on the front steps. In the house, they could see this guy named Archer sitting at his desk with a self-inflicted gunshot wound to his head. It looked like he'd shot the other four men then himself. He actually left a note on his desk telling the police where to find the other two bodies. As you can imagine, it's been a day at work with this call."

Olivia trusted him as much as he did her. However, he thought that his trust of late was a little less than she was to him. Since the call today, he'd been jumpy, too, not wanting to tell anyone what he was feeling or going through. Colby was sure that even if the murder-suicide hadn't happened that way, that was the way everyone on the scene was going to see it. Parker would make sure of it.

After dinner, the two of them decided to go see a movie. It was still light out enough that they figured they'd walk to the theater and enjoy some popcorn as well. He couldn't believe how much it cost to just see a movie but he was willing to pay it for a night of good conversation and fun. Colby didn't realize how much he needed this night just as he was dropping Olivia off at her place. She said it was a bad night for him to stay over, and he found that he was all right with that. He wanted a good night's sleep, and being at home would pretty much guarantee that.

At three-thirty, his phone woke him up. It took him three tries to get the person on the other end of the line to stop talking long enough that he could figure out what was going on. It wasn't until he was sitting on the side of the bed, a faerie with him, that he understood that he needed to go and rescue someone. From where, he wasn't that caught up yet, but he'd do it for the family.

"She's powerful upset." He told Crumble that he would to if he'd been arrested. "Not Arrested, sir, but she's a witness to a death."

"Oh, I thought that she was in jail. Didn't you tell me that she was in jail?" Crumble explained again he thought it was the forth time that while the woman was at the jail, she hadn't been arrested. Just the witness to a murdered human. Thinking he'd finally gotten it figured out, he drove them both to the police station and asked for Officer Colrain who had been in charge when Crumble had been there.

"Is she your master?" While he hated that word, he knew that it was the only one that the little faerie would understand when talking about the person he was supposed to be looking after.

"Nay, she is my friend's master. Darling was off tonight, and I was with her. I didn't see anything. She kindly kept me away from the murderer. But she asked me to get one of the Tuckers and you were the closest one that I knew to her." He was there because he was a Tucker and close. Better, he supposed, than being the one dead, he shivered.

"I don't usually go out on trips like this one, but Darling's wife just had them a baby, and he wanted to be there with her. Emma, the master understood and said it was fine by her to have another in his place. She's very nice, Ms. Emma. The others, your family has taken her under their armpits and want her to keep safe."

"It's wing, not armpits." Crumble looked confused and said that humans didn't have wings. Letting it go, Colby changed the subject. "So why am I here if she's not in trouble? I'm assuming that she had some kind of part in the accident?"

"Nay, she had nothing to do with it. Because of her magical truck, she stopped in time to not do more damage. She is very lucky, the officer said in that she didn't muck up—I don't know what that means—any more than it already is. It was three cars that slammed into one another."

Colby was getting more and more information and understanding less and less. He didn't have a faerie around all that often, but when he did, he knew them to be confusing and a little aggravating. It was why he had opted not to have one around him when he came here. He didn't want to have to spend all his time in trying to figure out what was being said.

Finding the girl was easier than he thought it might be. She wasn't in a cell but in one of the offices of the large stationhouse. There was a blanket over her head, and he could see water stains on the back of the towel. Entering the room with her, Crumble said her name lightly so as to get her attention.

~*~

Emma looked at the man after asking Crumble if he was all right. She might well have done that several times over the last few hours, but she couldn't remember. She remembered a lot that had happened, but talking about the little person who might well have saved her life, she didn't remember.

"Crumble said that you were near an accident." She nodded and told him that it had happened right in front of her. "I'm sorry to hear that. He said that several people were killed when the crash happened."

"I didn't hit the car by an inch. By an inch." She tried to calm her voice down. "We were coming up on the light when this man in a red SUV leaned out of his car and shot the man in the car beside him. Just pulled out his gun and shot the man. I'm assuming in the head because the windshield splattered with blood the moment I heard the sound of the gunshot."

The man nodded, but she thought that he was humoring her. Looking at Crumble, he still had spots of blood on his...tunic? Dress? She didn't know, but it was on him. Pointing it out to him, he did a little body shake, and not only was he cleaned up but he had on different colored clothing as well. Emma put her head down and closed her eyes.

"The police said that it was nothing more than road rage. When one of the cars tried to pass the one with the shot victim, he was shot, too. Like the man wanted to be first in the race, and he was going to kill anyone that got in his way." Someone asked, she didn't know if it was Crumble or the man if she'd been shot at, and she nodded before speaking. "He turned the gun my way even though I'm at least six feet above him. All the bullet did was ricochet off the front of the rig and hit his car. That must have pissed him off more because he was coming at me to my door to, I guess, kill me too."

The door opened behind her, and she didn't bother looking. Someone had been coming into the room since she was brought in a few hours ago.

When someone put their hand on her back, it was all she could do not to scream and cringe from the warmth. Every part of her was freaking out, and she didn't much care for it. Sitting up, she looked at the woman.

"I'm Bailee. We talked the other day." Nodding, she sat up higher in the chair she was in. "You're just fine, you know that, don't you? No harm came to you as I promised you and your mother."

"I should be dead." Nodding once, she sat down across from her, and that was when she realized that they were alone in the room. There was also a cup of what looked like tea in front of her with a few cookies on the plate. "That little guy. He snatched me back and did something to me to make sure I didn't die, didn't he?"

"Yes. Crumble is very good at his job of protecting people. You wouldn't have died, not from the shooting, but had the man been able to get you out of the truck before he was killed, he would have surely murdered you. He would have run over you with your truck and killed —" She put up her hand, and Bailee stopped talking. "You're all right, as I have said to you."

"It scared me. The way he looked like he

was just going to do what he did without anyone stopping him." Emma looked at Bailee. "My mom, does she know that I was...whatever I was?"

"She is aware only that there was an accident that you were no part of but only as a witness. Nothing more. I didn't think that it would do either of you any good for her to know everything right now." Emma thanked her. "I had no idea when you left yesterday that this would have happened. I only wanted to see how long it would be before you were to get to each of the stores along Taylor's routes. For returns, you see."

"I know that shit happens, but this was about as close as I've ever come to hitting anyone or even causing damage to anything since I've been driving." Bailee told her that was why they hired her. "Thank you. I'm assuming that I still have a job? I mean, why would you come all this way if I didn't...how did you get here so fast? Is it that magic stuff again?"

"Yes, the magic stuff." She knew that they had magic. Not that she wanted to believe it, but if she were to be in her rig right now, she could go to her bedroom and lie down on a nice king-sized bed. Get her things out of dressers or her closet and take a shower in her full sized bathroom that was tucked into the little spaces that were there for her. There was even a fully operating kitchen with a table and two chairs she could sit at should she want to have lunch while not driving. "You've decided to believe me when I tell you that we're magical?"

"Honestly? I have no idea what I want to believe. The living room in my rig begs me to say I believe you, but in my head, there are just too many things that tell me that there is no such thing as magic." She eyed her hard. "No one has to shift to make sure I understand that there are lion shifters either. I got that, too."

Bailee laughed and she didn't find any humor in her. Not any of them. If not for the contract, she might well have not worked for them had she not already signed it. There was something extremely strange about all the Tuckers, and she wasn't entirely sure that any of them weren't a little off their meds.

"Drink your tea, Emma. It'll make you feel better." She eyed the tea and then looked at Bailee when she laughed again. "I promise you there is nothing in it other than a bit of sugar. The cookies are just that. Cookies. Just have a few sips, and you'll see, you'll feel much better."

"The police are going to send me to the hospital. They're afraid that I've had a bit of trauma. They don't know that half of it. I feel like I've been put into a large rabbit hole and can't find my way out. You're not helping." She told her that she was trying her best. "Yeah? Well, it's not working. I don't even know…I'm freaked the fuck out right now."

"No, you're just still wondering how you can be alive when he shot you. He did, you know. Shot you twice in the head. But as you said, Crumble saved you and you're going to be just fine. Nothing happened that you can explain to the police. You understand that, don't you?" She said that they'd lock her away. "More than likely just put you in the hospital for a few weeks, but we can't have that, now can we? You have a good job, and it keeps you from getting hurt. I told you several times that we take care of those that we love."

She was, in the end, taken to the hospital. The man who had come in with Crumble when she was at the police station was hanging around a lot. Twice, the nurse had to ask him to move so that she could do something for her, but other than that, he didn't say much. He did look like he was pissed off, but she had enough on her mind right now not to be fucking with a stranger.

At two in the morning, she was released to go home. Where that was from where she was, Emma didn't know, but she wanted a good night's sleep and some food in her belly before she started driving again. She knew that she could do it, even after the scare, because it was something that she needed to do. Her mom had found them a home that she loved.

Emma didn't really care for the house that her mom had found for them. It wasn't ugly or anything, but it was too big. Three bedrooms wasn't all that large, but after living in the rig for the past five years, it seemed huge to her. It was the yard that she loved, she told her mom and she was already putting a garden in so that she could have some fresh veggies when she wanted them. Another perk was that she could park her rig in the driveway and it not be in the way of her mom's car that she'd gotten.

Someone had parked her rig in the parking lot of the truck stop. She wasn't too far out that she couldn't get to it without going through a lot of darkness but it was safe as far as she could see. No bullet holes or anything that she could see either.

"Do you have an extra blanket?" she asked

the man, his name was Colby if he needed a pillow too, not having any idea why he'd need a blanket. "I'm going to stay out here in my car to make sure that you're all right."

"I'm fine. It's stupid for you to sleep in your car when you have a home someplace around here." He told her he had a boat, too, that he could sleep in, but wanted to be close to her. "I don't want you to waste your time sleeping around here. I'm going to get into my rig, lock the door, sleep for about forty hours, and get up and start again."

"All right then." She tossed a pillow and a blanket at him. She was disappointed when he was able to catch them both but went into her rig and decided to forget all about him. He was an idiot if he thought that she was going to invite him into her place, especially after what happened that evening.

The bed was cozy and warm. Large enough for her to stretch out in, too. After getting herself situated, she thought a little about what Bailee had told her about lion shifters. And when she'd not believed her, she had her husband shift into his and lay across her lap. Emma had nearly wet herself when he did that.

But he had been beautiful. Never being this

close to a large lion, she was told that because he was a leader to a leap, he was larger than his brothers, even the older one. His mane was wonderfully soft and his fur along his face and nose wasn't anything like she thought it would be. The entire experience with him had been telling and a lot nerve-wracking.

Waking at sometime in the middle of the morning, she could hear voices and didn't bother with getting up. It was Crumble, and he was talking to one of his friends, she supposed. The little man had saved her life. The very least that she could do was to allow him to have company when he wanted it. Rolling to her side again, enjoying the comforts of her rig, Emma closed her eyes and went right back to sleep.

At noon, her alarm clock telling her the time, she got up. It still boggled her mind that she had enough room in her rig to have a stand-up shower along with all the other things. Washing her hair twice, she was ready to face the day and to see how many more miles she could get under her belt before she wasn't allowed to drive again.

"Hi." She looked at the man before it occurred to her that it was the guy who had wanted to sleep out in his car. Not that she would have allowed him to sleep in her rig, but she did let him come into her space when he told her that he'd gotten coffee and donuts. "I got a variety because I didn't know what kind you'd eat."

"They're donuts. What's not to like about them." She did get her a glass of juice, not caring for coffee at all. When she was settled into her seat across from the man, she finally remembered his name. "Colby Tucker. Crumble got you when I asked him to get one of the Tuckers. I guess I could have handled it myself, but I was freaked a little out."

"You were a lot freaked out, not that I blame you. It was a close call for you. I'm glad that you're all right." She nodded, finishing off her second donut in favor of conversation. "I was wondering if I could follow you to your next stop. Taylor suggested it, telling me that you might need a second pair of hands when you get to the last stop. I guess you're picking up bags for the grocery stores."

"Im not sure what I'm supposed to do with them. I thought I was bringing them back to the warehouse." Colby explained to her that they were going to break them down so that any one store wouldn't have too many to deal with. "I guess that makes sense. Yeah, I suppose it's all right if you follow me. Or you can just ride in the rig with me. I'm used to having my mom around, so you being there all the time won't be too bad."

"Gee, thanks." She finished up her breakfast and told him that she had to get some supplies. As soon as she got out of the rig, he followed her. Whatever floated his boat, she supposed. But she wasn't going to allow him to bother her too much. She really did have a lot to do today.

Before You Go...

HELP AN AUTHOR

write a review

THANK YOU!

Share your voice and help guide other readers to these wonderful books. Even if it's only a line or two, your reviews help readers discover the author's books so they can continue creating stories that you'll love. Log in to your favorite retailer and leave a review. Thank you.

Kathi Barton, a winner of the Pinnacle Book Achievement Award and a best-selling author on Amazon and All Romance books, lives in Nashport, Ohio, with her husband, Paul. When not creating new worlds and romance, Kathi and her husband enjoy camping and going to auctions. She can also be seen at county fairs with her husband, an artist and potter.

Her muse, a cross between Jimmy Stewart and Hugh Jackman, brings her stories to life for her readers in a way that has them coming back time and again for more. Her favorite genre is paranormal romance, with a great deal of spice. You can visit Kathi online and drop her an email if you'd like. She loves hearing from her fans. aaronskiss@gmail.com.

Follow Kathi on her blog: http://kathisbartonauthor.blogspot.com/